BY SHEILA GRAU

ILLUSTRATIONS BY ADAM REX

AMULET BOOKS
NEW YORK

THE BOY WITH 7 SENSES

7 SENSES 2

PUBLISHER'S NOTE: This is a work of fiction. Names, characters, places, and incidents
are either the product of the author's imagination or are used fictitiously, and any
resemblance to actual persons, living or dead, business establishments, events, or locales
is entirely coincidental.

Library of Congress Cataloging-in-Publication Data

Names: Grau, Sheila, author.
Title: The boy with 17 senses / by Sheila Grau.
Other titles: Boy with seventeen senses
Description: New York : Amulet Books, 2016. | Summary: A retelling of "Jack and the
Beanstalk" on the unusual planet Yipsmix, where every resident has synesthesia, including
Jaq, who travels through a wormhole to Earth, where he must rescue a fellow Yipsmixer with
the help of a kind Earthling giant.
Identifiers: LCCN 2015051081 (print) | LCCN 2016012675 (ebook) |
ISBN 9781419721199 (hardback) | ISBN 9781613120828 (ebook) |
Subjects: | CYAC: Fairy tales. | Synesthesia—Fiction. | Senses and sensation—Fiction. |
Magic—Fiction. | Giants—Fiction. | Science fiction. | BISAC: JUVENILE FICTION / Fairy
Tales & Folklore / Adaptations. | JUVENILE FICTION / Science Fiction. | JUVENILE
FICTION / Humorous Stories.
Classification: LCC PZ8.G7477 Bo 2016 (print) | LCC PZ8.G7477 (ebook) |
DDC [398.2]—dc23
LC record available at https://lccn.loc.gov/2015051081

ISBN: 978-1-4197-2119-9

ABRAMS The Art of Books
115 West 18th Street, New York, NY 10011
abramsbooks.com

Mere air, these words, but
delicious to hear.
—SAPPHO, GREEK POET

THE TASTE OF *W*

TO THE PEOPLE OF YIPSMIX, THE WORD *wipper* tastes like spoiled milk. It's a rotten and sour taste, which perfectly fits the rodent that bears its name. The wipper might look creamy white and furry, but it is the most sharply unpleasant animal on their planet.

To be fair to wippers, most *w* words have this sort of taste, unless the *w* is paired with *o-r*, as in *world* or *worm*. Those words taste earthy and fresh, like a rich mushroom soup. The word *wonderful* doesn't quite make the jump from disgusting *w* to delightful *w-o-r*. It has an average sort of taste, like white rice, which is a shame. Imagine—you describe something as *wonderful,* and the other person has to take your word for it because his mouth is telling him that it's boring.

But back to those annoying wippers, because everything that happened to young Jaq Rollop can be traced to the day the wippers showed up in his garden.

"There's no doubt about it," Jaq said at breakfast. "We've got wippers."

His mother and grandfather both winced at the word, as if it had struck them across the face.

"Great moons, no," his mother said.

"Chimichanga," Grandpa said, to get the bad taste of the word *wipper* out of his mouth. *Chimichanga* has a nice, meaty-crispy flavor.

Jaq lifted his pant leg and showed them the bite marks on his ankle. Wippers love to bite ankles.

His mother pressed some damp tea leaves onto the bites to stop the poison from spreading. Then she gave him a kiss good-bye and a lunch bag filled with tasty words written on a piece of paper that Jaq could read as he ate the very bland ripweed sandwich. The Rollops were poor; they couldn't afford fancy foods like lunch meats or juice.

✳

Young Jaq Rollop was in his seventh year of rudimentary school, which meant he was forty-nine years old. That's a little over twelve Earth years, or seventy-three and a half Epsidor Erandi years, for readers on those planets (Hello! And, *Erip nu!*). I'm not quite sure about the equivalent years on Zanflid, because of the complicated dual-sun situation and its extremely elongated elliptical orbit. Suffice it to say, in his species Jaq was medium-sized, and his second molars had just come in.

The Rollop family lived on a farm at the far edge of Cruxlump, where the land was baked by the sun and as dry as a stale cookie. They grew ripweed because little else would grow in that unfriendly soil. Ripweed tastes wonderful, or, rather, it tastes like the word *wonderful* tastes, which is boring.

Jaq also had a garden where he grew a few brickleberry vines and some vegetables beside their one-room house. He did most of the chores on the family's small farm because his father was gone, his mother worked all day at the hushware factory, and his grandfather had trouble moving because he was lazy.

Jaq plowed the soil, planted the seeds, and pulled the weeds.

He sold whatever he grew at the farmers' market, and his mom let him keep half of what he earned, which was barely enough to buy himself a large, sweet, double-shot, extra-hot saltmint drink with heavy whip on the way home from school.

He needed that sweet treat. Farming was hard work on a normal day. Farming on top of school and homework was painful drudgery. When you throw in a nest of wippers, it's enough to make a guy cry like a twenty-two-year-old.

The wippers took him by surprise that first morning. He was picking brickleberries for breakfast when he saw a flash of white scurry by his foot and disappear into the next row of vines. Jaq chased after it, but instead of running away, the small rodent turned around to face him.

Jaq smiled. The little critter was just a big-eyed bundle of white fluff, no bigger than his foot. It had a twitchy little nose covered with whiskers and floppy ears that perked up like curious lightbulbs. Just as Jaq was thinking about how cute it was, it sneered at him.

"You looking at me, farm boy?" it said.

"W-w-what?" Jaq was stunned. The wipper wasn't scared of him at all.

"Stop following me," the wipper said. "Jeez, you're going to step on my tail, you clumsy fat-foot."

As Jaq stood there in shock, another wipper snuck up behind him and bit his ankle. When he turned around to kick it, the wipper catapulted itself away, jumping higher than Jaq's head. *Boing!* As Jaq watched, a third nipped him from behind. They were small bites, and only mildly poisonous to Jaq, but after six or seven, it got really annoying.

After that, every morning and afternoon was the same. Jaq would go to work in the garden or in the fields, and the wippers would attack. He found that he was mostly immune to the poison of the wipper bite, but not so immune to the sarcastic taunts that flew out of the wippers like spit. Imagine a field of older siblings, popping up unexpectedly to insult your outfit, or that pimple on your nose, or to tell you that you throw like a toddler. That's what a field infested with wippers is like.

"Hey, dummy! I'm beginning to think you couldn't grow a weed in a field of manure," one would say.

"I know, right?" another would agree. "How hard can it be to grow brickleberries?"

"I bet he couldn't grow mold on an old piece of cheese."

"You did plant seeds, right? Pebbles don't sprout, in case you were wondering."

Jaq put out traps for the pests, but the very next day he

was served with a cease and desist order from the Wipper Protection Society. That's right, those pesky wippers are a protected species, which meant that Jaq couldn't kill them; he couldn't even rough 'em up a little. The members of the WPS are city folk who think that if an animal is cute, it can't possibly be a pest. As a result of this protection, wippers aren't afraid of farmers, because they know the farmers can't touch them.

There is only one animal the wipper is afraid of: the freasel, known affectionately by farmers as "the wipper-slinger." Jaq needed a freasel, but to get a freasel, he'd have to get permission from his mother.

And unfortunately for Jaq, his mother's favorite word was *no*, even though it tasted like fish paste.

2

THE WEIGHT OF WORDS

NO MATTER WHICH PLANET YOU LIVE ON, you're going to have to do some work if you want a pet of your very own. On Epsidor Erandi, it's a long process that involves allergy tests, training courses, home-safety measures, and a review of the child's crammed-full-of-activities schedule to see if there's room in it for pet care. If a child manages to make it through all that, then the desired pet is declawed and defanged, and purchased, along with a leash that matches the one the child has been wearing since he or she could walk.

Parents can be slightly overprotective on Epsidor Erandi.

I'm not entirely sure how kids on Zanflid get their pets, but I think it involves a trek through the jungle with a large bug and a can of net spray. The bug chews a path through the poisonous kufi plants, revealing the small bamu bears that dwell beneath them. One shot of net spray and—*swoosh!*— you've captured your first pet. If its mother doesn't eat you first.

On Yipsmix, much like on Earth, the first step in getting a pet is proving to your parent that you can take care of it. Jaq tried to show how responsible he'd be by looking after his grandfather so his mom could rest after a hard day's work.

"If I can take care of Grandpa," he told her, "a freasel should be a piece a cake." That was true. Not only was Grandpa lazy, but when he was upset, he also had a habit of angrily pointing at things and making everyone guess his complaint. This was annoying for all involved, even Grandpa, but he did it just so he could say, "You'll never hear me complain," and nobody could call him a liar.

To ease his mother's burden, Jaq jumped in whenever Grandpa got pointy: "The soup's too hot? The soup's too cold? The soup tastes like *wonderful* tastes? Soup shouldn't be that gray color?"

Grandpa frowned and pointed at his soup again.

"The bowl's too small? You want the purple bowl? Hmm. You're looking at me through the hole in your spoon. You want to play peekaboo? No? What is it? Now your spoon is leaking. Oh! You need a new spoon!" Jaq jumped up and got another spoon for Grandpa, then looked at his mom. But she simply said no.

Jaq knew that his classmate Wixlix had just gotten his own freasel, so Jaq asked him to come over after school. Kids didn't really like coming all the way out to the edge of Cruxlump, so Jaq had to promise to do Wixlix's homework for a week. When his mother was within hearing range, Jaq prompted Wixlix to talk about how great it was to have a freasel.

After Wixlix left, Jaq said, "See, Mom? All the other kids have them."

But his mom said no.

No is such a hard word to swallow.

Jaq kept trying. He made a little freasel shed out of wood he found by the river. He tucked the little home in a corner of the garden.

"A freasel could help me in the fields," he said. "I'll get more work done."

"No."

"Look at my ankles!" he shouted in desperation. His ankles were covered in red dots, the bites of the wippers. "And they make fun of my hair."

"The boy needs a freasel," Grandpa said. "Give them wippers a taste of their own medicine."

"Just ignore them," Mom said. "I'm sorry, Jaq, but we can't afford a pet."

Jaq saved his farmers' market money and tried to earn a bit more by helping out at other stalls. He gave up his after-school sweet drink—which he needed more than ever, now that he was doing three times the usual amount of homework. (His neighbor Tormy Vilcot had heard about his deal with Wixlix and made Jaq do his homework, too, or he'd tell.)

"I'll pay for its food," he promised.

"No," said Mom.

"Arrr!" Jaq threw his hands in the air. Of course his mother said no. She always said no. Whether he asked if he could go with other kids on a camping trip ("No, it's harvesting time.") or for new spiked shoes so he could play vargyball ("No, you already have a pair of shoes.") or for a little pet, it didn't matter. His mom would always say no.

Grandpa gave him a pat on the back. "When I was a kid, I had three freasels. Called them Cap, Milfrix, and Tammy. I had a hoverbike, too. Didn't realize how good I had it. Now it's all gone. Thanks to that farm-stealing Ripley Vilcot."

"Not helpful, Grandpa," Jaq said.

That night, Jaq sat in bed, thinking, *I just gotta have a freasel. I just . . . gotta . . . have . . . a . . . FREASEL!*

The next day, Jaq walked home from school with his head hung low, pulled down by the powerful gravity of all those *no*s. *No* is such a heavy word.

Tormy Vilcot rode past Jaq on his hoverbike. He turned in circles just to stir up the dust, and laughed. Needless to say, Jaq did not like Tormy Vilcot.

"When are you losers going to sell us that pathetic farm of yours so I can finally have the swimming pool my grandfather promised me?" Tormy shouted as he spun around Jaq.

Jaq didn't answer. He had no answer. His family had nowhere else to go.

"You know, I kind of like not having to do homework," Tormy said. "Maybe you should keep doing mine from now on."

Jaq ignored him, which just made Tormy laugh harder.

"How's the farming going? I bet it's hard to harvest when your ankles are being attacked, huh?" And then he laughed again and sped off for home.

Of course, Jaq thought. Tormy—no, probably Tormy's grandfather—had planted the wippers in their field. The Vilcots had been trying to buy the Rollop farm for years, but Grandpa refused to leave. If there was one thing Jaq hated more than those horrible Vilcots, it was . . . well, nothing, because he really hated those horrible Vilcots.

As he neared home, Jaq passed the Vilcots' massive farm, with its mechanical harvesters and its herd of mantelopes, which gave the tastiest milk on all of Yipsmix. Grandpa's voice played in his head: *When that was my farm, we didn't just have mantelopes. We had robuses, caponutters, and gows, too.*

"Not helpful, Grandpa," Jaq said to the voice in his head.

Jaq, already beaten down by all those *no*s, felt his head sag even lower at the thought that the Vilcots would tear down his home just so Tormy could have a swimming pool. At home, he crouched over his three sets of homework, taking breaks only to rub out painful hand cramps.

He slumped through his work in the field, getting his

ankles nipped by those pesky wippers. But drooping over like that just meant the wippers got a better look at his head.

"Honestly—that hair," one of the wippers said. "What do you cut it with?"

"Safety scissors, I bet," said another.

The rest laughed.

"I bet he cuts it in the dark," said another. "With nail clippers."

They howled with laughter.

"I bet he uses a stapler," another one said.

This was followed by an awkward silence.

"That doesn't even make sense, Bonip," the first one said. "You can't cut anything with a stapler."

"I know, I know," the one called Bonip said. "Um, a hole puncher?"

"I'm going to pretend you didn't say that," the first one said. "Now I've lost my flow." He rolled his shoulders, did some shadowboxing, then said, "Hey, kid, I saw another guy wearing that same shirt. It's amazing how different it looks on someone with muscles."

The wippers roared with laughter again.

By the end of the day, Jaq's head felt so heavy, he just plopped it on the table and slurped up his plain noodles while his mom tried to spice them up with a poem by Niviax Wormager. She wrote the most delicious poems, using words like *luminous* and *bungalow* and *elixir*.

Grandpa patted him on the back. "When I was a kid, I had a butler who fed me when I was worn out from riding bungee-cycles all day," he said.

"Not helpful, Grandpa," Jaq muttered. "You know, I think the Vilcots planted the wippers here. Tormy as much as said so on the way home from school. He wants us to sell so he can have a swimming pool."

"Never!" Grandpa shouted, slamming his fist on the table. "That farm-stealing Ripley Vilcot is NOT getting this land. I'd pluck my eyeballs out of my head before I'd let that happen. We're not leaving!"

That was easy for Grandpa to say. He didn't have to face the wippers twice a day.

3

15 IS A VERY RUDE NUMBER

THE NEXT DAY, JAQ STOPPED AT THE PESTS-B-Gone Emporium on his way home from school. (The one in the marketplace, not the one out by the hushware factory.) Mostly, he wanted to avoid Tormy on the road home, but he also wanted to see the freasels.

He'd wanted a freasel ever since he'd heard the name, with its cuddly *free* sound that tasted like pasta smothered with melted cheese. Even looking at the word on the wall gave him a warm feeling inside, until he saw the price.

The freasels were 15 damars each. 15 is an obscenely

tall and smug number. It's the kind of number that doesn't care if it hurts your feelings. To the people of Yipsmix, every number has its own personality, which is why they take great care in using them. By pricing the freasels at an arrogant 15, Pests-B-Gone was saying, *These animals are too fabulous for the likes of you.* And that made people want them even more.

Jaq sighed. He couldn't afford a freasel. He couldn't even afford a pair of extra-thick socks to protect his ankles, and they only cost a cheerful 2 damars each. The best he could hope for was some free advice on how to control the nasty biters. Lucky for him, Pests-B-Gone had a help desk, so Jaq got in line behind two farmers. He listened as they talked about their own pest problems.

"My winnowberry vines are covered with caterpokers," the first farmer said. "They're destroying my crop. I can't get rid of them."

"You can pluck 'em off with tweezers," the second farmer said. "It's tedious, but if you get rid of the queen, the rest will die. Me, I got critter moles that are eating up all my green leafies."

"My aunt had critter moles," said the first. "She tried everything—traps, poisons, nets. Nothing worked. Someone suggested getting a giant fang–toothed worm, and let me tell you, that did the trick."

"What happened?"

"The worm devoured those critter moles. Just ate 'em all up. Did a splendid job of aerating her soil, too. As soon as the field was clear, the worm's handler lured it out with some fresh meat, and her fields were ready for planting."

"Sounds expensive."

"It was a few hundred damars past expensive, my friend."

The men seemed knowledgeable, so Jaq decided to ask them for advice. "Are you talking about garden pests? 'Cause I got a bad case of wippers, and I don't know how to get rid of them."

The two farmers bolted away from Jaq as fast as they could run, which might seem rude, but they didn't even want to hear the word *wipper* for fear of Contagion by Mention, which is a thing on Yipsmix. You overhear someone talk about something, and before you know it, you've caught it, too.

Jaq watched them leave and shrugged. At least he was at the front of the line now. He stepped forward, and the woman behind the desk looked at him with her eyebrows raised. Jaq leaned in and whispered, "I've got . . . you know," and he reached down and pinched his ankles. "And they tease me."

The woman nodded. "These freasels have all been trained to sling the . . . you-know-whats."

"I can't afford them."

"We have some extra-thick socks to protect your ankles," she offered.

But Jaq didn't hear her. He was still gazing at the freasels. Their glossy fur, the little chirp sounds they made, the way their long bodies looked like tightly wound springs. He stood there for a few minutes, until he felt the woman watching him.

He shrugged and turned to go.

"Wait," she said, coming around the counter. "I shouldn't be telling you this—my boss doesn't like me sending customers away—but there's a guy I know. His freasel just had a litter of frips. One of them is a runt, and he says he's going to let it die. I told him he couldn't, and he told me if I wanted to save it, I had to take it. But I can't bring home any more animals. Here." She wrote down his address. "Tell him Kithorly sent you."

A huge smile burst across Jaq's face. "Thank you," he said. "Thank you so much!"

✳

"He's just a runt," Jaq said as he showed the tiny creature to his mother and grandfather. "A farmer was going to let him die. He might not even survive."

"Jaq!" His mother was angry; he could tell by the way red splotches appeared on her neck. "I told you, no pets!"

"I'll feed him myself," Jaq said. "You won't have to do anything. Mom, please. Please let me keep him. You know I wouldn't say please unless it was really important." The word *please* had a sweet, oily taste. It was the kind of word that got really annoying if it was used too much.

"He won't live through the night," Grandpa predicted. "Sorry, kiddo."

"Please," he said again, wincing. "I'll never ask for anything again."

"Darn it, Jaq," his mother said. "I wish I didn't have to come home to more problems. I have enough of them at work."

"Please, Mom," Jaq said. "Having a freasel—it's my dream come true."

"I dream of getting my land back from that farm-stealing Ripley Vilcot," said Grandpa. "But a little pet is nice, too, I guess."

The baby freasel was so small and frail that Jaq was afraid to touch him. He scooped up the little frip as if he were picking up a thin-shelled rickle egg, the kind that cracks if you so much as breathe on it.

He was so beautiful, with reddish-brown fur, a white belly, four stubby little legs, and two arm buds popping out of his front shoulders. So tiny!

Jaq's chest filled up, up, up with joy.

"What are you going to name him?" Grandpa asked, leaning in for a look.

"Klingdux," Jaq said. He'd had the name picked out forever.

"Like the superhero?" Grandpa said. "Good choice."

Jaq didn't sleep a wink that night; he sat up watching Klingdux, willing the tiny creature to keep breathing.

"You're a superhero, little buddy," he whispered. "You're stronger than anything."

He dripped milk into Klingdux's mouth from a spoon whenever his new pet woke up, but mostly the little critter slept.

Live, Jaq begged. *Please live.*

4

THE SOUND OF CRYING IS MAROON—IT DANCES AROUND UNTIL YOU NOTICE IT

B Y NOW YOU MAY HAVE NOTICED THAT Yipsmixers don't sense the world in quite the same way as most people do on Earth, or Zanflid, or Epsidor Erandi. Yipsmixers taste words. They see numbers as having both color and personality. But that's not all; they also see sounds. To them, sounds have color and shape and movement. Some people on Earth have senses like this, and it's called *synesthesia*. This extrasensory ability doesn't have a name on Zanflid or Epsidor Erandi.

When a Yipsmixer looks at a tree filled with chirping

birds, those chirping sounds make tiny blasts of red appear, like exploding apples. Listening to music is like watching a flowing tapestry of light and color that swirls through a person's vision. And the sound of crying looks like jumpy tangles of maroon floating like streamers.

Jaq's first night with Klingdux was filled with jagged maroon streaks that woke him whenever he drifted off to sleep. He didn't mind, though, because crying meant that Klingdux was still alive.

Jaq watched his pet carefully over the next few days. He noted which colors swirled out of Klingdux when he whimpered, growled, or hissed. Most Yipsmixers are very good with animals, because they communicate with all their senses. Jaq not only heard every noise his frip made—he saw and tasted and felt those noises, too. He soon learned that a whimper that filled his vision with frothy orange bubbles meant hunger. Yellow blasts meant pain. Velvety purple swirls meant "Play with me." Sometimes the whimpers were so faint, he couldn't hear them, but he saw them.

He listened and watched and tasted and learned, and he kept Klingdux alive.

Weeks passed, and Klingdux grew bigger and stronger. During those weeks, Jaq braved the merciless herd of wippers every day, telling himself that soon, soon, his freasel would be ready.

Jaq shared everything with Klingdux: his food, his narrow bed in the corner of the one-room house, and his blanket. He used his farmers' market money to buy special freasel food. Taking care of Klingdux made Jaq feel capable and happy, especially in Rumbletime, when the skies thundered worse than an angry Vilcot who didn't get to cut in line at the carnival. Klingdux would curl his shaking body next to Jaq, making Jaq feel like the brave one. He was the best friend Jaq had ever had.

Klingdux grew stronger every day. He was quick and agile on those four short legs. His long, sleek body scurried and twisted through the house, which wasn't a problem until his arms grew in. As soon as those little arm buds on his front shoulders lengthened, the baby freasel started grabbing anything he could reach. He'd clutch his prize, then spin around like a discus thrower and sling it across the room.

Jaq smiled and laughed at his frisky pet. "Isn't he fantastic?"

His mother rolled her eyes. His grandfather shook his head and mouthed the word *no*, but Jaq didn't see that.

After Klingdux broke two cups, a plate, and his mother's

reading glasses, Jaq made a ball out of rags and let Klingdux sling that. Soon the thumping sound of the rag hitting a wall filled the house whenever Klingdux was awake.

"Enough!" his mother screamed one evening after a long day at the hushware factory. "I want that little ball of destruction out!"

"But, Mom," Jaq said. "He's too small. He's not ready."

"You put him outside or I will," she said, her neck turning purple. "He's woken me up every night, and I can't take it anymore."

Jaq's heart fell, but he picked up his pet and headed outside with his blanket. He wasn't going to let Klingdux sleep alone. They curled up on the back porch together and slept.

The next morning, Jaq woke up with the sun. Klingdux slept peacefully next to him, wrapped in the blanket. Jaq stood and stretched.

"Klingdux, I really don't think you're ready for this," he said.

Klingdux popped up, his lithe body swiveling in happiness.

"Those wippers are so fast and vicious. And you're so small." Jaq walked to the edge of the porch and looked out over the ripweed field. The stalks seemed to be shooing him away as they swayed in the breeze, as if they were warning him of danger.

Klingdux followed him to the edge of the porch. "Stay," Jaq commanded, holding up a hand. Klingdux sat down and waited.

Jaq prepared to enter the field. The ripweed stalks were as high as his waist. He looked back at Klingdux, who was watching him intently. Jaq swallowed over a lump in his throat. He hoped Klingdux was ready, but what if he wasn't? What would those wippers do to him? There were so many of them, and only one Klingdux.

Jaq stepped into the field. The morning was quiet, and Jaq could feel his heart thumping. *This is it*, he thought. *This is what he's meant to do. He can do it.*

But what if he can't?

Another step. He sensed the eyes of the wippers on him. He imagined they were taking their time, letting him suffer in suspense as they thought up the perfect insult. Suddenly, panic flooded his body. He couldn't do this to Klingdux. Klingdux wasn't ready.

Jaq turned to go inside. But it was too late.

"Oh, look—it's the kid with bangs." A wipper had cut off Jaq's route back to the porch. When Jaq turned around, he saw that he was surrounded. He'd fallen into their ambush. "You ever think about shaving the whole mess off?"

"Yeah, bald is in," said another.

The sound of wipper laughter filled the air.

"Not with that head," another said. "He'd look like a melted snow cone."

More laughter.

"Or a half-filled balloon, waiting for more air to lift it up."

The other wippers agreed. And laughed.

"Or . . . um . . . a bald kid with a misshapen head."

This one was followed by silence.

"Good grief, Bonip. Use a simile or something."

"Sorry. Um . . . like a green leafy cabbage, except not green, or leafy, or cabbage-y, but the same roundish shape? And then, um, sort of squished?"

"Somebody hit him for me," said the first.

As the wippers fought among themselves, Jaq looked back at Klingdux, who was shaking with desire to run into the field. He'd seen the wippers. Jaq could tell he wanted to sling them.

"Let's bite his ankles," one of the wippers said, and Jaq felt a sharp pain by his foot. When he swung around, another attacked from behind, just like always. They hopped away from his kicks with tremendously high jumps. It was as if they had powerful springs in their hind legs. They were infuriating.

And they were everywhere. Jaq couldn't take it anymore, so he shouted, "Klingdux!"

Swift as a sandstorm, Klingdux raced off the porch and into the field, his long body twisting around plants. He swooshed through the stalks, sneaking up on the nearest wipper and grabbing it with his long arms. He whirled about in a tornado of spinning, and then—*whoosh!* He let the wipper fly.

It was a spectacular display of athleticism. A thing of beauty! Like watching a wrestling match of graceful dance moves.

"Look out! Wipper-slinger!" the wippers cried.

Jaq could feel the panic of the wippers as they scurried and hopped, but Klingdux was just too fast. He ran them down and threw them, again and again. And when the wippers jumped into the air to escape, soaring higher than Jaq's head, Klingdux would track their flight and be waiting when they landed. And then he'd sling them over the plants and across the field, and, if it was a really good sling, the wipper would hit a tree and fall down—*splat!* They always shook themselves and got back up, but the tree-hit wippers took a little longer to return.

Jaq smiled so wide, his face hurt. Sure, those pesky wippers would be back. They always came back. But he'd have at least a couple of hours to work in peace, and that was just fine. Klingdux could just sling them again. Over and over.

It was the best, happiest morning of Jaq's life.

5

THE HIGH FREQUENCY
OF ENVY

SOMEONE ELSE WAS WATCHING JAQ'S FREA-sel work, and that someone was Jaq's next-door neighbor, Tormy Vilcot. From his second-floor room in the very house that used to belong to Jaq's grandfather, Tormy could see right down into the Rollops' field. And because he had no homework to do, he had plenty of time to stare out the window and dream about swimming pools.

Every day, Tormy Vilcot watched Jaq walk to school with his wipper-slinger. He watched Jaq walk home with his wipper-slinger. He watched Jaq laugh and run and play with his wipper-slinger. And when he had nothing to do because Jaq was doing his homework, Tormy Vilcot watched that beautiful freasel sling wippers. It made him laugh out loud—until he realized something.

Jaq Rollop has a wipper-slinger, and I don't.

Tormy Vilcot's ears started to ring. They buzzed and hummed like a tornado, or a fly he couldn't swat away. Tormy didn't like that droning buzz.

When Jaq came over with Tormy's homework, Tormy offered him ten damars for his wipper-slinger, but Jaq laughed in his face.

"Twenty damars?" Tormy offered.

"Klingdux isn't for sale," Jaq said. "Why don't you go to Pests-B-Gone? They've got a bunch of them there."

Tormy didn't want a freasel from Pests-B-Gone. He wanted Jaq's freasel, and he wanted Jaq to have no freasel. That was two wants buzzing in his ear, and he couldn't stand it.

"I'm doing you a favor, you dumb lump," Tormy said. "With twenty damars you could buy another freasel yourself and have enough left over to get some new clothes." He pointed to Jaq's shirt. "The Cruxlump Warriors aren't even a team anymore. They folded twelve years ago."

"Sorry, but he's not for sale."

✳

Ringggggggggg, buzzzzzzzz.

Sometimes the whine in Tormy's head would go away, but it would zing right back if he saw Jaq or the wipper-slinger, or if someone said the word *homework*, which tasted like seaweed and reminded him of Jaq and his wipper-slinger.

Tormy felt assaulted by this reverberating ring. It made him very irritable. No one would have noticed the difference, because he was always irritable, but now he was violently irritable. He punched walls, he kicked fence posts, and he screamed at his family.

His parents tried to bribe him with sweets. They tried to appease his envy with toys. They bought him a new pet of his own, a rare and expensive tippi bird. None of it worked.

"I WANT THAT WIPPER-SLINGER!" he screamed at dinner.

His grandfather, the wealthy Ripley Vilcot, placed a shiny gold package on the table.

"Is that what I think it is?" Tormy's mother said, her whole face beaming with fake-surprise happiness.

"Yes," his grandfather replied. "And it cost me more than my new Arbian foal."

"Oh, Tormy, you are such a lucky kid," his mother said.

"It's glug!" She reverently pushed the small box closer to Tormy. "You can't buy this at the marketplace. You have to know someone. Your friends will be so jealous."

His grandfather unwrapped a piece of his own glug and popped it into his mouth. He chewed and chewed, and then blew a huge bubble. When it popped, the noise made a burst of yellow stars appear in Tormy's vision. They looked like they were shooting out from his grandfather's face. Tormy's mother laughed and clapped her hands.

"Not every kid gets to chew fresh glug," his grandfather said. "You can pop bubbles in your friends' faces. And think of all the things you can do with a nicely chewed wad of glug. That's valuable stuff, right there. You could save it, and someday you'll have enough for your own soundproof glug room! Or add it to your glug trophy display. Or—"

"I don't want glug!" Tormy screamed, snatching the pack and shoving it in his pocket, because he did want it. Glug was one of the most valuable things on Yipsmix—who wouldn't want it? "I want that wipper-slinger!"

His grandfather clenched his teeth and blew out through his nose. He seemed to come to a decision. "Then you shall have it," he said. "No Vilcot goes without."

6

SPEAKING WITH YOUR HANDS IS EASIER WHEN YOU WEAR THE RIGHT GLOVES

THE NEXT DAY, RIPLEY VILCOT PUT ON HIS riding gloves—the everyday pair, not the fancy evening pair, or the casual pair, or the "Don't mess with me, I'm angry" pair—and climbed onto his prize-winning Arbian mount. He rode out of his stable and down his driveway. From there, it was a short hop down the road to the Rollops' farm. Arbians are fantastic hoppers.

This place would make a perfect annex to my farm, he thought, looking at the Rollops' measly spread. *I could tear down that one-room shack they call a house and build a gazebo, draped with* winnowberry vines. I could replace that pathetic garden with a nice lawn, and bulldoze that ripweed field and put in Tormy's pool—maybe with a statue of me in the middle. It would be so much more pleasurable to look out on myself, rather than this dry and dusty eyesore.

The Rollops' home *was* squalid, and it looked like the roof was ready to cave in. Weeds curled around the base of the house like greedy fingers. Faded shirts hung on the clothesline, waving as if they were saying, *Save us from this desolation!*

How long do I have to wait for them to leave? Why won't they sell me this worthless blip of land?

Vilcot knocked on the door with his gloved hand, wondering if he should have worn the "Don't mess with me" pair instead.

Jaq's mother answered.

They stared at each other.

Vilcot thought that Mrs. Rollop really should take better care of herself; she was a mess. Her eyes were droopy, and her hair was graying and frizzy. It looked like she hadn't had her nails done . . . well, ever.

"Mrs. Rollop," he said at last.

"Mr. Vilcot," she replied.

"It is your great fortune," he said, smiling, "that my

grandson has become enamored of your farm's freasel. I am prepared to offer you a price well in excess of what they are charging at Pests-B-Gone. I think twenty damars is more than fair, and you should accept it. Obviously"—he looked around her and into the room—"you need it."

He opened his wallet and began counting out the bills.

"I'm sorry, Mr. Vilcot, but Klingdux belongs to my son, and he's not for sale."

Ripley Vilcot had had a feeling she wouldn't accept his first offer. She was so obvious in her greed. He decided to feign surprise at her rejection.

"Really? Are you sure? It's a very generous offer."

Mrs. Rollop shrugged. She was doing some acting of her own, Vilcot could tell. The old "It's out of my hands" bit. He blinked at her, wondering how best to proceed against this greedy woman.

"Very well," he said after a few dozen blinks. "Twenty-five damars. But I assure you, I will not go one damar higher."

"I'm sorry," she said. "Why don't you buy one at Pests-B-Gone yourself?"

Vilcot was stunned into silence. It was an angry silence. A silence that poked him in the ribs and told him he was losing. Whirls of black and gray appeared at the edges of his vision, haloing Mrs. Rollop so that it looked as if her head was framed in menace. Vilcot had seen this picture before; it happened whenever he thought someone was trying to take advantage of him. If there was one thing Ripley Vilcot would not stand for, it was someone who thought she could play him for a fool.

And she's playing me, he thought. *Of course she's playing me. Oh, how I hate the Rollops! I hate them. I hate the type of people they are. They relish being troublemakers, they do. It's the only satisfaction they get out of life, spoiling better people's lives. Just because they're incapable of achieving any sort of success themselves.*

The swirls of black were now streaked with red, and they shook as if they were laughing at him. Vilcot imagined Mrs. Rollop telling the other workers at the factory, *Look how much the old fool paid for my wipper-slinger!*

It took him a moment to unclench his teeth and say, "I see. I will give you one last chance to accept my generous offer. I don't think you want to refuse it."

"I'm sorry."

You will be.

Vilcot turned to go. *Nobody laughs at me. I will not let her get away with it.* And then he struck his mount much harder than necessary and hopped home.

A plan formed in his mind as he left the Rollops' struggling farm. *They'd be a little more eager to sell if their crops failed,* he thought. *Oh, yes . . . if I divert the river, their farm will get no water. It will cost me a fortune, but sometimes a lesson has to be taught. Nobody will say no to me again.*

7

WORRY PRICKLES THE BACK OF YOUR ELBOW

A FTER DINNER, JAQ LISTENED AS HIS mother recounted her confrontation with Ripley Vilcot.

"There's something not right with that man," she said. "You talk to him, but he stands there twitching and fidgeting like a schoolboy about to have a tantrum."

"Was he wearing his 'Don't mess with me' gloves?" Grandpa asked.

"I don't think so. They were just normal gloves."

"How insulting! He doesn't even think we are worthy of

his best gloves. Thought we'd be a pushover for his wheeling and dealing."

"Did he try to buy the farm again?" Jaq asked.

His mother and grandfather didn't answer. They looked at each other, like they were hoping for the other one to talk. Jaq's gaze went back and forth between them.

"He doesn't want the farm," his mother said at last.

"What *does* he want?" Jaq asked. Klingdux was curled up next to him on the floor, and Jaq stroked his soft fur. Then he noticed Grandpa looking at Klingdux.

"No," Jaq said softly. "No, he can't."

"He offered twenty-five damars for him," Mrs. Rollop said. "Think of what we could do with that money, Jaq. Better irrigation for the fields, fix the roof, repair the drafty floorboards."

"You don't hear me complaining," Grandpa said. Then he pointed to his blanket, because he felt a draft and didn't want to get up.

Jaq fetched the blanket and then rushed back to Klingdux. "He's the only friend I've ever had, Mom."

"I know," his mother said. "We won't sell him to that man."

Jaq was relieved, but later, as he lay in his corner of the room, he heard that sentence a different way, and in this new way, *We won't sell him to that man* didn't mean that they wouldn't sell him to someone else.

On Yipsmix, emotions are heard and seen in addition to being felt. That night, Tormy Vilcot sat at home, his ears ringing with envy. His grandfather paced in his office, anger swirling red and black in his vision. And Jaq lay in bed, his elbows prickling with worry.

Jaq wasn't sure he could trust his mother. He knew she didn't like Klingdux. She never had. He began to imagine her snatching up Klingdux while he slept and then selling him to Vilcot. Anger popped to the surface of his vision, like underwater bubbles, and burst open. The thought that she could be so treacherous was very real to Jaq, and very frightening.

She never let him have anything he wanted, and now she was going to take away the one thing he loved. It wasn't fair.

Many planets set aside a special day to celebrate mothers. It's a day when young children can show their love through handcrafted art projects. On Earth, young children sometimes make a necklace out of colored macaroni, or decorate a picture frame, or draw a picture using their handprints as flowers. The gifts are adorable, and mothers love them.

On Epsidor Erandi, macaroni would be considered a choking hazard. Picture frames, with those sharp edges, are too dangerous for kids to handle. And they would never allow their children's hands to be painted—how unsanitary! Instead, most children sing a song for their mothers, usually about the importance of safety, or how much they love wearing a helmet as they walk to school.

To honor their mothers on Zanflid, young children take their machetes and venture into the jungle to collect the venom of the poisonous tree snoogli. It's a great gift because the venom is very useful in making medicines and perfumes, and it's relatively easy to extract. Tree snooglies hardly ever hear you sneak up on them. Mostly never.

On Yipsmix, children collect the clear rocks they have nicknamed "foot scrapers" because of their hard, sharp edges. Teachers help their students polish the foot scrapers, and then they are given to mothers on Gratitude Day. The worthless rocks are very pretty once polished. When the sun hits them, the clear stones light up with rainbows of color.

Jaq had just passed a nice-looking foot scraper on the path as he walked to the river, but he didn't pick it up. Usually, he collected as many as he could find, saving them up for Gratitude Day, but he wasn't feeling very grateful for his mother at the moment. The last few mornings he'd woken up wondering if this would be the day she would make him sell Klingdux.

He continued down the path, kicking away a few more foot scrapers and swinging the bucket he was going to fill with worms for the garden. But when he got to the river, the river was gone. There was nothing left but a dry depression in the land. He checked his gravity irrigation lines, and they were dry, too.

That was strange. The river had never run dry before. Ever.

He walked up the riverbed and immediately saw why: The river had been moved. Jaq had seen the massive earth-moving equipment working behind the Vilcots' spread; he had assumed they were digging a swimming pool or clearing land for another field. But no, the Vilcots had dug a massive trench, and the water now flowed down to them before taking a wide swing away from the Rollops' farm.

Without water, Jaq's crops would wither and die.

✳

And they did.

Over the next few months, the Rollop family struggled.

Almost all of Mrs. Rollop's factory wages went to pay off the loans they'd taken out to buy the land and seeds. They really needed the crop money to buy food, but the crops failed.

They grew very hungry.

At breakfast, which was a half bowl of ripweed oatmeal topped with one brickleberry, Jaq's mother broke the bad news.

"Jaq, I don't think we have a choice anymore. We have to sell your freasel."

"Mom, no," Jaq said. "He's mine. I can't . . ." His voice trembled, and he felt body-shaking sobs rise up inside him.

"Then we'll all die of starvation together," Mom said, angry now. "Is that what you want?"

Jaq hugged Klingdux a little tighter.

"You've trained him well; he's grown so big and strong," she said. "I'm sure he'll fetch a good price. With twenty-five, thirty damars, we can dig a well for your irrigation system and be ready for the next planting. I'm sorry, I really am, but he's just a pet."

Just a pet? Jaq's world burst with explosions of sadness. Gray streaks swished through his vision and wound around his throat, making it feel tight.

Grandpa put a hand on his shoulder. He didn't say

anything, and that was when Jaq knew there was no escaping this terrible fate. He was going to lose his best friend.

"I'm not selling him to Tormy Vilcot," he said.

"No, of course not," his mother said. "His grandfather was back yesterday, saying he would take him off our hands for twenty damars. He said the offer went down because he could see that we're desperate. He's an awful, evil man. Diverting our water so he can steal a pet for his spoiled brat of a grandkid."

Jaq hugged Klingdux and cried.

8

THE TASTE OF *X*

THE LETTER *X* TASTES LIGHT AND SPRINGY and sweet, which is why the letter *X* is so popular when naming things on Yipsmix. Ending a word with an *X* is like topping a cup of hot chocolate with a dollop of whipped cream. Delightful.

The name *Xenoth* starts with an *X*, but because it sounds like a *Z*, it bears none of the wholesome goodness of *X*, and neither did the man named Xenoth.

Xenoth knew that when he wrote his name on a piece of paper, it looked purple and golden and trustworthy, but when he said it out loud, people's faces turned cold, and they immediately said words such as *Transfix* and *Victory* to get the bad taste out of their mouths. Nothing tastes sweeter than *Victory*.

Xenoth was a cunning fellow, so he changed his name to Davardi, and people would say his name just to taste it. It didn't change the fact that inside he was as greedy and untrustworthy as the number 48.

Now this greedy man who had renamed himself Davardi was sitting at a sidewalk café in the marketplace when he spied Ripley Vilcot looking around frantically. *What can the crazy old codger be up to now?* Davardi thought. *And is there any money in it for me?*

"Davardi," Vilcot said. "There you are. I have a job for you, if you're interested."

"Always interested," Davardi said, carefully dabbing his mouth. "If it's worth my while."

"Good," Vilcot replied as he took the seat across from him. "Now, this is a small job. My neighbor is going to be desperate to sell his wipper-slinger. A wipper-slinger that my grandson would like to have."

"Let me guess—the neighbor isn't feeling neighborly? He doesn't want you to have it? Gee, Vilcot, you still don't know how to make friends, do you?"

Vilcot sneered and leaned closer, whispering, "I want you to buy the wipper-slinger. I offered him twenty damars. I'll go as high as thirty. You bring me the wipper-slinger, and I'll give you a little bonus."

"Fifty damars," Davardi said. "That's my fee." There was a beautiful leather jacket and matching boots he'd seen in the window at NM Clothiers. He really wanted that jacket. He would look so good in that jacket. He couldn't sleep at night for wanting that jacket.

"I'll give you forty damars," Vilcot said. "That will give you thirty for the animal, and ten for you. Honestly, you could do this in the time it takes to brush that hair of yours." That was actually an understatement. In the time it took Davardi to brush and gel and properly shape his black hair, he could probably buy a freasel, run a mini-marathon, and teach a class on proper glove accessorizing.

Davardi knew that Vilcot was a prideful man, a man who had to believe he won every negotiation. And the stubborn Vilcot was wearing his "Don't mess with me" gloves. Davardi had a few pairs of those himself. He would have to proceed very carefully to get what he wanted. And what he wanted was fifty damars.

If Davardi came right out and demanded even one damar

more, Vilcot would leave and find someone else for the job. And Davardi didn't want just one damar more; he wanted fifty damars, and he thought he knew how to get it. He was a con man, after all.

"I'm not trying to be hard, Vilcot, but I need fifty damars," Davardi said. "I've got a job lined up in East Lumlox, and if I'm late to show up, they'll dock me. Listen, we've worked together before, and you've seen that I can be trusted. I get the job done, and I don't talk. Sometimes people in your position reward that kind of loyalty, and people who reward loyalty are greatly admired. Like Klingdux the superhero—when he finds a trustworthy ally, he rewards him handsomely. And everyone admires Klingdux."

"That's true," Vilcot said, nodding. "You've proved yourself trustworthy. You know, I have been compared to Klingdux before."

Sure you have, Davardi thought. *By me, when I was buttering you up on my last assignment.*

"All right," Vilcot said. "I'll give you fifty damars. You keep twenty."

Davardi nodded, suppressing a smile at how easy that had been. "What makes you think this kid is going to be desperate to sell?" he asked.

"I've made him desperate to sell." Vilcot smiled. "Nobody plays me. That's the lesson here."

I'll try to remember that, Davardi thought, stifling a chuckle. *Now I just have to get the kid to hand over that freasel for nothing.*

9

SADNESS, SADNESS, SADNESS, EVERYWHERE YOU LOOK

THE NEXT MORNING, JAQ COULDN'T TASTE his breakfast or his mother's cheerful, "Good morning, sweetie, sweetie, swift and speedy." His mother often tried to cheer him up with *S* words because they tasted like feathery candy melting in your mouth, but today Jaq was too sad to notice. He didn't hear the early birds chirping or see the colors of their tweets swirl in the air. His brain couldn't think of anything except *I'm losing Klingdux*.

He loaded his best friend into the wagon and fastened his collar. He didn't feel his legs start to walk, but they did. As they passed the sideyard and Jaq's small garden, he didn't notice that his brickleberries looked small and deflated, like they were sad, too.

He did hear the wippers, though.

"The swift monster is tied up!" one shouted. "Look, everyone, the skinny kid is defenseless."

Jaq would have let it go. He wasn't going to work in the garden; he was leaving. *Just ignore them and move on.* That was his motto, most days. But this was not a day to pick on Jaq Rollop. He was already feeling as low as a person could feel.

"You're so skinny," another wipper said, "when you go for an X-ray, I bet they just take your picture."

The rest laughed.

"Aw, sling it," Jaq said. "One last time, little fella. Go get those wippers." He untied Klingdux's leash and sent him into the garden.

Jaq watched Klingdux work and felt his throat tighten again. He didn't want to lose Klingdux, and not just because he could sling the sarcasm right out of those wippers. Who would walk with him to school in the morning and then wait for him outside? Who would curl up in his lap when he did his homework? Who would make working in the fields not only bearable but fun, too?

When all the wippers had been slung, Klingdux returned to Jaq and wound his way around his ankles like a silky scarf. Jaq put his collar back on and loaded the freasel into the wagon. Wiping a tear from his eye, Jaq set off.

It was a long road to the market. The sky was the color of 9, a deep purplish blue. It hung over him like a threat. He'd been hoping for a cooler, misty blue, like the number 37, but it wasn't his day, in more ways than one. Klingdux sat in the back of the wagon, looking at their farm.

Jaq walked on, the sepia tones of his world not bursting with colors the way they would if he had someone to talk to, or something to eat, or if someone was cooking something nearby. Yipsmix is a world of muted colors—browns and tans and sages and grays. His senses provided the colors, and his senses were dulled by sadness.

"Klingdux," he said. His pet looked up at him. "Aw, Klingdux, I'm so sorry. Mom says we'll starve if we don't get some food. You're the best freasel ever. I don't want to sell you, but I have to." He choked up a little. "I'll work extra at the farmers' market. I'll get you back. I promise I will."

Halfway to the marketplace, someone rode up behind him. Jaq braced himself, expecting a Tormy dust assault, but it wasn't Tormy. When he turned around, he saw an elegantly dressed man riding a deluxe hoverbike that seemed to float on a whisper. Even the bell on his handlebars sounded expensive.

Ping . . . la-di-da!

So fancy.

"That a wipper-slinger?" the man asked. He took off his helmet, and Jaq saw the most perfect hair he'd ever seen in his life. His jaw dropped at the sight of that hair. So wavy and precise, all the hairs in perfect formation.

Until the wippers had arrived, Jaq had never paid much attention to hair. He knew his hair was a bit scraggly and long, but he'd always liked it that way. He didn't want to look like Tormy, with his short, neatly parted hair. This guy, though, was something else. *Wow, to have hair like that.*

Jaq nodded, hypnotized.

"Nice," the man said. "My name's Davardi, by the way. Are you selling that wipper-slinger?"

"Huh?" Jaq knew the man had asked him something, but he didn't hear anything after the word "Davardi." The name filled his mouth with the most magnificent flavor.

"Are you selling that wipper-slinger?" the man asked again, smiling. He had perfect teeth, too.

"Yep. My mom says I can get thirty damars."

"In your dreams," the man said with a friendly smile.

He was right. Jaq's mom had told him to settle for twenty-five but to start higher.

"Listen," the man said. "How about a trade?"

"Nah, I need the money. For food." Jaq rubbed his belly.

"And when the food's gone, then what? No, what you need is opportunity." He dismounted and walked over to Jaq. "That's what I got. I got so much opportunity, it's busting out of my pockets. Why, look here."

He held an old-fashioned key with a long shaft. One side was roundish, filled with curlicues; the other had notches that were square and precise, like mathematics. It was a graceful combination of logic and whimsy, and Jaq thought it was beautiful.

But it was just a big key.

Trade my wipper-slinger for an old key? Not likely, Mr. Perfect.

"It's a special key," the man said. "Opens the market's VIP pantry. You've seen the place, I'm sure. Back behind the restaurant supply depot?"

"Right," Jaq said. "I've seen that place." He'd always wondered what was in that big building. He pictured stacks of hushware plates and platters, though, like his mom made at the factory. All the best restaurants used hushware, so that forks and knives didn't make that clinky-scrapey sound on a plate when people were eating. That kind of sound ruins an otherwise delightful meal.

"They only give out, like, seven of these keys. It entitles the owner to free access to all that food. The place is never empty. Me? I got all the food I need. This key is worthless to me. But I do have a giant wipper problem. I'm desperate. Pests-B-Gone is all out of freasels. Your mother will be very proud of you when she sees this."

Jaq thought about it. If this pantry thing was true, then he could surprise his mom and grandpa with loads of food. They'd be so happy. And then he could collect food and sell it, maybe making a few damars a week. It wouldn't take long to earn enough to buy Klingdux back. Maybe.

But something didn't feel right. Couldn't this guy get a whole lot more than a freasel for that key?

"I think I'd better just go to the market."

The man got on the bike. "Your loss. But I understand— you're a kid. Gotta do what Mom says, and make no mistake! In a few decades, you'll be ready to think for yourself." He put on his helmet. "You know, everything I have, I got it all because I made a deal like this once. And when you've made it and are a huge success, like me, it's nice to give something back to those less fortunate, don't you think? Let others have the chance that you had. Well, take care." He smiled, and the bike lifted into the air.

He was leaving, just like that. He didn't really care about trading. He was just a nice and generous rich person, and Jaq was letting the opportunity of a lifetime slip through his fingers.

"Wait!" Jaq said. "I'll do it."

His mom would be so proud. Jaq knew it.

Jaq could tell by the way Mom hurled a plate at the wall that she wasn't even a tiny bit proud. She tossed the key out the window, and Jaq was sent to his corner bed without any rip-weed broth, which was how she sent herself to bed, too. That made Jaq feel worse than his head lump.

What had he done? Not only had he lost his best friend, but he'd let his mom down, too. He felt so stupid. So, so stupid. Humiliation and pain cramped his insides, and he couldn't sleep. Tears rolled down his cheeks as he looked outside. It was one of those bright nights where one moon was full and the other moon was half full, and it looked like the sky was winking at you. Jaq felt as if the whole world was mocking him, even the great sky god, Smolders.

He went to sleep listening to the sarcastic insults of the wippers outside his window, and he believed every word they said.

The next morning, Jaq woke up hoping it had all been a bad dream. But when he looked out the window, he saw the key still on the ground, where his mother had thrown it. It had broken in half.

He climbed out to take a closer look and discovered that it wasn't really broken—it was supposed to open. There was a hidden compartment inside.

Jaq picked up the pieces. *Dead wippers! There's a note.* He carefully unrolled the piece of paper that was stuffed inside. It read:

My dear Greggin,

I haven't heard from you in years, so I can only guess that my written reports are getting lost in your office because you are such a busy and successful man. But I know you would never ignore a message in a key, so please, please take heed.

Things have gotten dicey on my expeditions, and I only narrowly escaped last time. But I must return. I told my man that if I wasn't back by Great Smolders Day, then he should take this key and deliver it to you personally. If that has happened—if you are reading this—then I am in need of rescue, and only a man of your resources and unwavering courage can help me.

I promise it will be well worth your while. I've collected amazing riches on this spectacular, giant-filled planet called Earth. Our precious glug is everywhere. On the roads! Under movie theater seats! Stuck beneath their enormous shoes!

The map on the other side will show you to the gate. Find the wormhole. It will bring you here. Look for the building with two enormous golden arches. It's a glug mine! I should be nearby. Find me!

Yours,

Plenthy

Jaq read the letter three times. How odd. He looked at the map on the back. He recognized some of the landmarks: the marketplace, the river, the hills.

Was this some sort of joke? A gateway to another planet? One that was filled with giants and glug? It sounded like a science-fiction story. Jaq knew there were no such things as gateways to other planets. Or glug mines. Imagine!

Jaq laughed.

But then he thought: Who wrote this note? What if he really was in trouble? And had that swindler known about this note? Jaq couldn't even think the name "Davardi," because it was so delightful, and the man was clearly not. He would refer to him only as the Swindler from now on. But if the Swindler had seen the note, wouldn't he have kept it?

No, Jaq concluded, he couldn't have known about it.

Amazing riches, the note said. Jaq often dreamed of being rich, of buying his grandfather's farm back from the Vilcots. Or making enough damars so his mother didn't have to work so hard. But did he want to travel to a giant-filled planet? No, he did not.

What if he offered this note to the Swindler in exchange for Klingdux? That was all that Jaq really wanted. Maybe that man would be interested in a glug-filled world, as outrageous as that sounded.

About as outrageous as a pantry of free food. That was stupid. How did I believe that?

Still, it wouldn't hurt to try. Jaq decided to track down the Swindler right away.

10

THE SMELL OF FOOD IS
LIKE A WARM BREEZE

I T WAS EARLY, SO JAQ PICKED A BOWL OF brickleberries and left them on the table for his mom and grandpa. Then he put the key and note in his backpack and headed out.

He had just reached the front gate when he stopped and shook his leg.

"Are you going to let go now?" he asked the wipper clinging to his ankle. "I'm leaving, and I won't be back for a while."

The wipper unlatched his jaw and looked up at Jaq. "Take me with you," he said.

Jaq shook his leg harder, trying to dislodge the pest. "What? No! I hate wippers."

"Please? Pretty please? Gorgeous please?" The little fellow looked so pathetic, with his long white ears flopping down and his big, sad eyes.

"Why do you want to come with me?"

"I'm a terrible wipper," he said. "My insults are lame, and I can't bite ankles very well." It was true. He hadn't even broken the skin on Jaq's ankle. "The other wippers tease me."

"You get teased by wippers?" Jaq said. "Gee, what's that like?"

"It's terrible."

"I was joking. I know what it's like."

"Oh, right," the wipper said. "So you know how I feel. You have to take me with you. I won't be a bother—I promise. I'm quiet and well-mannered and potty-trained."

"What's your name?"

"Bonip."

"You're the one who said I cut my hair with a stapler?" Jaq asked.

Bonip nodded.

"Yeah, that was bad." Jaq laughed. "Okay, you can come."

Bonip asked to ride on Jaq's shoulder, and Jaq let him.

The wipper was smaller than Klingdux, but having him there reminded Jaq of his pet. It was a bit of a comfort on the long walk until . . .

"You ever think about doing something different with this stuff?" Bonip asked. His tiny paws were combing through Jaq's shoulder-length hair. "Like washing it, maybe?"

"Shut up about my hair," Jaq said.

"You're right. And you should keep it long. It takes attention away from your nose."

"It's funny that you think you're bad at insults."

"I'm working on it. Was that a good one?"

Jaq shrugged, which sent Bonip off his shoulder and to the ground. He bounced back up, smiling, because wippers are used to being flung, and they are practically indestructible.

Jaq walked with Bonip leaping beside him. They made it to the marketplace, where the scrumptious smells of roasting food and sweet candy seemed to brush against Jaq's skin. The food smells curled and spun around him politely, as if they were saying, *Allow us to introduce ourselves.* The feel of food was everywhere. Everywhere except in Jaq's stomach.

The marketplace was a hushed collection of quiet stores carefully constructed to keep everyone from being overwhelmed by their senses, which happened whenever large groups of people came together. There were smells, but they were subtle and they melted away on a breeze provided by silent fans. There were noises, but the streets were cushioned and stores were equipped with noise-canceling devices that sucked up sound. There were sights, but the colors were muted and the shapes were straight and predictable. People kept conversation to a minimum while shopping, careful not to bombard their fellow shoppers with unsavory tastes or unappealing colors.

Jaq entered this peaceful zone, passing stores selling food, stores selling home decorations, stores selling clothes, and toys, and all sorts of things. Stores with trustworthy addresses and fun and joyful names you could taste when you said them out loud. The marketplace had wide lanes and sidewalk tables for eating. In the middle, there was a big open space with a fountain and benches. Jaq loved the fountain. The hushed burbling of the water created gentle streams of color that filled the air around it. It was like watching fireworks.

As he approached the fountain, Bonip scurried up Jaq's leg, his back, all the way to his shoulder. The wipper's fur was sticking straight out, making him look much larger than he was, and really fluffy.

"Let me in the pack. Let me in the pack. Gorgeous pleases. Please, please, please."

Jaq hated wippers, so he lifted his pack into the air, out of Bonip's reach from where he was perched on Jaq's shoulder.

"Please, please, please," Bonip begged. The little wipper was in a complete panic. "Bad man over there. Please."

Jaq noticed a group of men over by the fountain. He lowered his pack, and Bonip scurried inside, popping his head out to point at the man. "Him."

It was the Swindler. Sure as sunlight, it was him, standing next to his fancy hoverbike.

"Why do you think he's a bad man?" Jaq asked.

"He kidnaps wippers from their families in the wild and dumps them into random fields with lots of other wippers. Then he comes by to sell the farmer a wipper-slinger, and the farmer is desperate, see, so he pays extra. Then the poor wipper is slung to kingdom come every morning, noon, and night. And when he's not being slung, he's off crying because the sophisticated farm wippers make fun of the poor country wipper."

"You?"

"Me? No. Just a guy I know."

"Right. Hide in the pack if you want, but I've got to talk to that guy. He has my Klingdux."

"The swift monster," Bonip said in an awed whisper.

"Yeah." Jaq smiled. "I've got to get him back."

Klingdux was nowhere to be seen, but the Swindler had a fancy new jacket and matching boots. Jaq guessed he could buy a used hoverbike for what they'd cost. He could hear the Swindler talking as he approached.

"Genuine gow leather—feel how soft. It feels like smelling freshly baked bread during a sunrise. Go on, feel it."

The man he was talking to reached out to touch it, but the Swindler slapped his hand away. "Don't touch it. Just imagine something really soft. It's like wearing a cloud."

His friends looked on with awe. The Swindler smiled. He was chewing glug, and he blew a giant bubble, popping it in front of the guy's face. Then he laughed. "Who wants to buy my glug?" He took the wad of chewed-up glug out of his mouth and held it up. "All nice and chewed. Ready for business."

A bidding war erupted as people offered him money for his glug. It was a nice-looking wad of glug, Jaq had to admit. With enough of it, a person could make a soundproof glug room. All the great palaces and mansions had glug rooms. Jaq sighed just thinking about it. Imagine, no stray sounds drifting in to taint your senses with unpleasantness. You could fill the room with whatever sounds you wanted—a buffet of music, a soft quilt of chimes, a vista of melodies.

"Sold!" the Swindler said, and the exchange was made. The crowd dispersed, and Jaq drifted over.

The Swindler looked up. "Oh, great," he said. "It's the stupid kid." He turned to walk away.

"Hey," Jaq said. He pulled out the key. "I want my freasel back."

The Swindler turned around. "Sorry, kid. A deal's a deal. Besides, I already sold the squirmy little beast."

"Sold him?"

"Yeah, you think I wanted him for myself? Please. Feel this jacket. No, don't touch it. Just imagine what an expensive jacket feels like. Does a person who wears a jacket like this need a freasel?"

"You tricked me," Jaq said.

The man shrugged. "And it was so easy, too. But, hey, you learned something, didn't you? Think of it as an expensive lesson in not trusting strangers. You can thank me later."

"Where's Klingdux? Where's my freasel? Please, Mr. Swindler, I've got to get him back."

"Listen, kid, your freasel is gone," he said. "Go buy

another one. I don't think his new owner wants to sell. He went to a lot of trouble to get that animal."

Jaq's heart sank. "Vilcot."

The Swindler chuckled. Jaq watched him as he drifted off on his hoverbike, laughing like a maniac.

Tormy Vilcot had Klingdux.

Oh no. Jaq felt like his heart had been yanked out of his chest, thrown on the ground, and then trampled by that evil kid. How was he going to get Klingdux now? Tormy didn't care about money. He had so much of it already.

Maybe, after Tormy had Klingdux for a while, he would get bored with him and sell him back. Maybe Jaq could get another wipper-slinger and pretend like he was happier than ever, and Tormy would want to trade. No, that might hurt Klingdux's feelings. He could never do that. Besides, Klingdux was the best wipper-slinger in the world. Who would ever want to trade him?

Just a stupid kid like me.

Jaq realized that losing Klingdux was only one of his problems. He and his family were still hungry. He had to find a way to get food, and he knew there was only one option left.

He had to go to the wormhole and find this glug-and-giant-filled land called Earth.

11

A YELLOW DAY IS A
GOOD DAY FOR A QUEST

O N EPSIDOR ERANDI, GOING ON A QUEST
is a youthful rite of passage. It comes after the
"Giving Up the Blankie" rite of passage (which
can take years) and also the "Sleeping Without the Night-
Light" rite of passage (also years). During the "Quest" rite
of passage, the adolescent is given a map, a compass, and a
bag of healthy snacks. The child is then led into the backyard
and told to find his or her way back to the house. Often, the
parents are waving from the back porch, to make certain
that their offspring makes it back safely. Successful child-

ren are awarded trophies and hugs and told how clever they are.

Adolescent quests aren't really a thing on Zanflid, but sooner or later every kid gets snatched by a wild zaroopka on the way to school. The many-tentacled beast then stuffs the kid under a log while it fetches its babies for mealtime. Kids usually get away before they're eaten. The zaroopka has a terrible sense of direction and often forgets where it stashed its food.

Earth is a bit of a mixed bag when it comes to youthful quests, and on Yipsmix they're actually discouraged. Nevertheless, Jaq left the marketplace and embarked on one. He didn't really want to, but he had no other choice.

He walked down a road shaded by tall lem trees. The trees had dark brown trunks and sage-green leaves that whispered in the breeze. The sound of rustling leaves made soft blue dots appear in the branches, and it was pretty. But Jaq wasn't really paying attention. He was looking at his map.

If he followed this road, eventually it would take him to the trailhead for the Manguno Laguno Nature Preserve. There, a series of trails crept up into the amber-colored hills. Somewhere up in those hills was a wormhole that led to Earth.

"I'm hungry," Bonip said, peeking out of the backpack. "You didn't pack any food in here."

"No, I didn't," Jaq said. "Mellifluous, unique, haberdashery."

"Say what?" Bonip said.

"I'm hungry, too."

"So you speak nonsense?"

"Those words taste good to me," Jaq said. "Rimple muffin."

"How about 'Wonderful wipper woefully hungry'?"

"I don't like those *W* words. Or words that start with *B*."

"Like . . . Bonip?"

"Your name tastes like fish-flavored bark, with a sour aftertaste," Jaq said. "It's revolting."

"Well, excuse me. I'm not very fond of 'Jaq' myself. It's too short for a name. But I guess that suits you, shorty. Plus, you smell bad."

"Why don't you go home?" Jaq said, stopping to look at the pest, which was hard to do, because he was still perched on Jaq's backpack. "I'm not in the mood to be insulted. Badly."

"I'm sorry," Bonip said, climbing onto Jaq's shoulder. "But you started it. I don't want to go back. To be honest, the other wippers won't even have noticed I've been gone, and that will make me feel worse than starvation. Can we get something to eat, please, please, pretty please?"

"No," Jaq said. "And by the way, when you say 'please' over and over, it grates on my nerves like someone chewing with their mouth open. It makes me want to scream, it's so annoying."

"Oh? Sorry, then. Can we get something to eat? I beg of you? I beseech you? Pretty beseeches? No, 'pretty' probably tastes bad, too . . . Gorgeous beseeches?"

"How about you don't plead for anything."

"But I'm hungry."

"I'm hungry, too."

They walked on.

*

"How much farther?" Bonip asked a few steps later. He'd collapsed in a dramatic heap, draping himself over Jaq's shoulder. "Are we there yet?"

"Does it look like we're there? I'm still walking."

The road had come out of the trees and into a neighborhood with square houses sitting behind neat gardens. The gardens were filled with calming colors, the kind of colors that didn't take a side in an argument, because they were neutral.

"Where are we going?" Bonip asked.

Jaq looked at the map. He had reached the spot where the street curved to the left and the trailhead was up on the right. "I'm going to try to rescue a guy who needs help and hopefully get myself some glug at the same time. But first I have to find something called a wormhole. It should be up this mountain."

"Wormhole?" Bonip said, perking up.

Jaq had given a lot of thought to this wormhole. He wondered if he'd be too big to fit into it, but at the same time he really hoped it wasn't the hole of a giant fang-toothed worm, because a giant fang-toothed worm would eat him.

Jaq, being a farmer, loved worms. The small ones. They were a gardener's helpers, loosening and fertilizing soil. Whenever Jaq had a day off from school, he would go to the river with a bucket and collect as many worms as he could. Then he'd carefully place them in his small garden, and in the fields, too.

"A wormhole sounds perfect," Bonip said. "I could really go for some worms right about now. That's one thing I can say about your pathetic garden—it's loaded with worms."

"You guys eat my worms?" Jaq asked.

"Huh? *Your* worms? Um, no."

Of course they do. Great Smolders, Jaq hated wippers! He brushed Bonip off his shoulder. The wipper landed with a bounce and looked up at him. Jaq pointed at Bonip. "It takes me hours to . . . Oh, forget it! Don't follow me. Just . . . *don't.*"

Jaq stormed off, not looking back. If he had looked back, he would have seen a sad little wipper with a quivering lower lip watching him leave.

Jaq reached the mountain trail and pressed onward. His legs were weak and shaking from hunger, but his anger kept him moving. He held the map in front of him, looking for the landmarks that were mentioned.

"There's the broken tree," he said to himself.

"There's the rock that looks like a face," he said a little later.

"There's the river. I'm getting close."

He crossed a rope bridge where the river was wide and calm. Then he followed the trail that led to the waterfall. Soon, the playful river was lapping and splashing over boulders. The sound made dots and swirls appear in Jaq's vision. Twice, he veered suddenly, as if he were dizzy.

Jaq wasn't used to walking next to so much sound. He knew the dots and swirls weren't really there, but they startled him. Like most youngsters on Yipsmix, he was still learning how to filter out unnecessary sensory information.

The constant rush of noise grew louder as he climbed the trail. The splashing of the river seemed to echo off the trees next to it. Jaq's vision became more and more clouded with blasts of color. Rounding a bend, he was met by a cascade of sound that completely filled his vision. To Jaq, it looked like he was walking toward overlapping strips of color, but he was really walking toward a steep embankment next to the raging river, a river that could sweep him away and smash him against giant boulders if he fell in.

And that embankment was just one step away.

12

HE'S STRONG, HE'S SWIFT—HE'S KLINGDUX THE INDESTRUCTIBLE!

A FOOTSTEP FROM DISASTER, HE HEARD A scream.

"Stop!"

Jaq froze.

"What's wrong with you?" Bonip screamed. "You're about to fall into the river!"

"I can't see!" Jaq said. "It's too noisy!"

Bonip climbed up to Jaq's ear. "Listen to my voice. Take three steps back."

Jaq did. Bonip guided him back around the bend, where

the sound of the river was more muted. Once they were safely away from the river, he jumped off Jaq's shoulder.

"What do you mean, you can't see because it's noisy?" he asked.

"The sound of the river—it throws blasts of color in my vision."

"Jeez, Bigleg," Bonip said, shaking his head. "First *B*s taste like fish and now waterfalls make colors appear?"

"Yes," Jaq said. "Don't you taste and see sounds?"

"Nope. I only see things that are there. Sounds come in my ears. Smells come in my nose. I taste food when I have some in my mouth, and I feel things that touch me. That's it."

"You're a strange little fellow," Jaq said. "It's like your brain is stunted, and it just experiences one sensation at a time. You only have five senses?"

"Yeah. How many do you have?"

"Seventeen."

"Shut up."

"What? Everyone does," Jaq said. "Sense of direction, sense of time, sense of motion, sense of pain, sense that somebody is watching you—" He stopped listing them to wave away an orange ribbon of sound as a bird cawed from the branches above.

"Yeah, *I'm* the strange one," Bonip muttered.

Jaq blinked. He rubbed his eyes. "I'm never going to make it to the waterfall."

"Can we move away from the river?"

"No, there's only one trail," Jaq replied. He put his hands to his temples, closing his eyes again. He breathed deeply and tried to relax. He knew that with fixed concentration he could focus on the important sensory information. It was what they learned to do in school.

Soon he was able to make the colors fade to the edges of his vision enough so that he could continue up the trail. "I think I'm okay now," he said. "I'm going to try that bend again."

Bonip looked at him, his hands clasped together, a questioning look on his face.

Jaq sighed. "You can come. And . . . um . . . thanks for saving me . . . you know . . . by the river."

Bonip bounced cheerfully and then climbed onto Jaq's shoulder. "Give me the map. You close your eyes, and I'll guide you."

The path grew narrower and steeper as they continued. The crash of water raged louder and louder. Even the thumping of Jaq's heart was clouding his vision now.

"We're almost there!" Bonip screamed over the noise of

the falls. "It looks like the wormhole is behind the waterfall, and the waterfall is right there!"

Jaq nodded. They crept along slowly because Jaq was very nervous walking next to that powerful surge of water with his eyes closed. One misstep and he could slip in and be rushed away.

"Step forward!" Bonip yelled. "Another step! Another! Doing great! Three more steps! Now stop! Turn to the left! Okay—forward! Forward!"

Jaq could feel the mist on his face. The trail turned muddy and squishy, but he kept following Bonip's directions. And then, suddenly, the thunder of the waterfall sounded a bit muted. Jaq risked opening his eyes. He had to blink a few times because he was in a dark cave.

"Where are we?"

"Behind the waterfall. The cave entrance was right there. I walked you inside a few steps, and then the cave turned, and here we are."

Jaq pulled out his map, but he couldn't see anything. He continued down the cave because there was nowhere else to go. Soon the walls closed in and he could touch both sides with his hands.

As he neared the end of the cave, he noticed a faint glow.

An oval shape was shimmering at the end of the tunnel. He inched closer to get a good look. It was unlike anything he'd ever seen before. It seemed to give off a faint hum that radiated beautiful bright curlicues of color. It was hypnotizing and exotic.

"Dead end," Bonip said sadly.

"Are you kidding? It's right here!"

"Where? I can't see anything."

"It's practically exploding with color," Jaq said. "I can feel it vibrate when I move my hand close."

Bonip ran down Jaq's outstretched arm to see if he could feel it, too, but this startled Jaq and he shook his arm. Bonip flew into the air, his momentum carrying him forward, right toward the strange, glowing space. And then, *zip!* He was gone.

"Oops," Jaq said.

13

AN ASSAULT ON
JAQ'S 17 SENSES

B ONIP?" JAQ CALLED.

Nothing.

"Bonip? Come back out!" Jaq shouted at the shimmering oval.

Bonip remained gone. He had disappeared into the wormhole. Was that a bad thing? Was it a good thing? Had he jumped through a portal to Earth? Or had he just been eaten by a strange new species of giant fang-toothed worm?

I have to follow, Jaq thought. But all of a sudden, he really didn't want to. He had never been a jump-in-first kind of kid. He was the kind of kid who made sure the water was deep enough, warm enough, and free of bloodsucking creatures and harmful chemicals before he jumped in.

Jaq knew he had to go after Bonip. The wipper needed his help, probably. Or maybe not. The little guy was shifty and resourceful. *Maybe I should wait and see if he comes back out. That would be the wise thing to do. Right?*

No, he should be bold and go after him. Jaq knew that without great risk, there is no great reward. Grandpa had told him that once, right before he'd taken a nap.

Grandpa was right. He should jump in.

But Grandpa had lost his farm because of a bad investment. Should he really take advice from him?

Jaq paced with indecision. He walked toward the wormhole, persuading himself to jump in, only to spin away as arguments against jumping in popped into his head.

Just step through. It's why you came here.

No, wait—it could be dangerous. Hunger can be beaten. Dead is dead.

Jump, you coward!

Don't be foolish!

You really don't have a choice, Jaq, a third voice in his head told him. *You have to jump. It's what Klingdux the superhero would do. And probably Klingdux the freasel, too.*

Jaq closed his eyes, held his breath, and stepped forward.

He was sucked into the wormhole. The rocky walls of the cave seemed to disappear into emptiness. As his world faded away, he felt a strange sensation, like his body was being squeezed and pulled apart at the same time. The air was sucked out of him, and he couldn't breathe, couldn't speak. All was silent.

At last, he burst free and fell onto soft soil. Before he could get up, Bonip jumped on his face.

"What took you so long?" Bonip asked.

Jaq inhaled with relief. "Where are we?" He brushed himself off and stood up. He seemed to be in a forest of tall plants with giant leaves. "How did we get here? What's going on?"

"Isn't it great?" Bonip said, peeking through the leaves. "Have you ever seen colors like these?"

Jaq looked through the leaves and immediately knew one thing for certain—he wasn't on Yipsmix anymore. Gone were the soft browns and muted grays of his home. He'd landed in a brightly colored, screaming nightmare. It was an alien world filled with explosions of sounds and colors and smells.

He'd never experienced anything like it, and it made him dizzy.

"Focus, Jaq. You're spinning," Bonip said.

Jaq plugged his ears. He tried to calm himself, because it's very hard to concentrate when your body is jittery with panic. If sadness dulls the senses, then panic magnifies them. He breathed deeply and recited the prime numbers up to 503. All prime numbers were soft and round and kind. They were like friends who helped him relax when he was frightened.

"Concentrate, concentrate," he chanted to himself. "Two, three, five, seven, eleven—"

He peeked out of the bushes. They were in a place that seemed similar to the marketplace on Yipsmix, but all the stores were indoors and stacked on top of each other, two stories high with a roof over everything. The sounds and smells and sights were trapped inside. They bounced around angrily, like wild beasts trying to escape. They seemed to charge right at Jaq, and he wanted to turn around and dive back into the wormhole.

And then he screamed. Two giants were walking by his hiding spot in the plants. Jaq had known that he was going to see giants—Plenthy's letter had called this place "giant-filled." But knowing and seeing were two different things.

These giants were massive.

Jaq covered his mouth and ducked back behind the protective cover of the plants.

"Winking moons, they're huge!" he whispered to Bonip. "Let's get out of here."

"Wait," Bonip said. "Jaq, we came here for a reason. Just relax. Take it slow. The wormhole is right there. We can dive back in if we have to, but let's see what's going on here."

Jaq felt his whole body tremble. He looked at Bonip, standing so bravely at the edge of the plants. "You're right," he said. He took a deep breath and tried to calm himself again. "The wormhole's right there."

They were well hidden in the little border of plants, so Jaq peeked out again, fingers back in his ears. His neck craned upward as another giant walked past. Jaq guessed that he would come up to the giant's midcalf. He was surprised at how similar they were to Yipsmixers, the only real difference being their size.

The plants were neatly contained in an area edged by smooth, shiny bricks. High above Jaq a glass ceiling filtered light down onto a sparkling fountain in the center of the space. A couple of giants sat at the edge of the fountain while others walked past. Storefronts faced him from the opposite wall.

The fountain murmured and crashed with noise and, in Jaq's view, popped and swirled with color.

Bonip jumped onto Jaq's shoulder and poked him in the cheek. Jaq unblocked that ear.

"There's got to be food nearby," Bonip said. He pulled on Jaq's shirt. "Do you smell that?"

"I smell everything," Jaq said. "Don't you have any senses that are going crazy?"

"Just one," Bonip replied. "My sense of hunger." He punched Jaq on the cheek again. "Hey, you're losing it, guy. Focus! We need to find food. Just block out all that other stuff and focus on food smells. C'mon, Jaq. It's not that bad. What if I stuffed some dirt in your ear?"

Jaq replugged his ear and sniffed.

Oh, man, this is hard. It took a lot of concentration to suppress his other senses. He felt like he was shutting off chunks of his brain, but doing so brought relief. His vision cleared enough to see what was really in front of him.

And there, on the facing wall, just to the right of the fountain, he saw them. The golden arches that Plenthy had mentioned in his note. Two of them, just like the letter had said. "There." Jaq pointed. "We have to go over there."

"Okay!" Bonip said. "Let's go."

"We should wait and watch first," Jaq said.

"Bonip doesn't wait and watch first," Bonip said. "Bonip goes after what he wants."

And with that, Bonip jumped off Jaq's shoulder and onto the bricks that bordered their little forest of plants. He hopped down to the ground and started across the open space.

Every bit of Jaq wanted to crawl back to the wormhole and go home. Every bit except the tiny little part of his brain that he'd forgotten to shut off. The part that told him he should never, ever, abandon a friend.

Bonip wasn't exactly a friend, though, so it was a murky area.

14

FRENCH FRIES TASTE ROUND

B ONIP WAS JUST A SPECK TO THE GIANTS. They didn't notice the white fluffball as it dodged their steps. They would notice Jaq, though. He was sure they would.

He tried to swallow, but he had no saliva left in his mouth.

"You coming?" Bonip called. He had reached the edge of the fountain.

Jaq took a deep breath. "Okay," he said to himself. He stepped onto the brick edge of the plant area. The drop to the floor was only about half as tall as he was. He waited for a trio of giants to pass, and then jumped down. He ran out, quickly covering the space between the plants and the edge of the fountain, where Bonip waited. He grabbed the wipper and hurried to the next bit of cover, a potted tree outside the golden-arches store.

Once safely in the shadows behind the pot, he leaned on his knees and waited for his body to stop needing air so fast.

"Why did you stop?" Bonip said. "I see food in there!"

It was true; there were long yellow food sticks on the floor next to a red box, and the aroma coming out of the restaurant nearly knocked Jaq over.

He was so hungry. But he was looking at something else— a sticky blob on the ground next to him. He bent down to investigate. He gasped.

"What?"

"It's glug! The letter was right—there are big blobs of glug all over!" Jaq's heart leaped with excitement. "Do you know what this means?"

"It means I have to wait here while you tell me, instead of going in there and sticking my face in that red box of delicious-smelling food."

"It means my troubles are over," said Jaq, who was pulled out of his daydream of riches by smells so delicious, so enticing, so real that his mouth started to water. They drifted out of the store's doorway and tiptoed right up his nose. "Okay—I'm heading for that table. We can hide behind that silver pole holding it up."

He ran, and when he got there, he gasped again. "Look up, Bonip! It's a glug mine. Look at all that glug!"

Stuck to the underside of the table were at least ten huge globs of glug.

"If every table has this much glug, imagine . . ."

Bonip didn't say anything. In fact, Jaq realized that his shoulder felt lighter. He turned around and saw Bonip out in the open, eating a pale yellow stick he'd found on the floor. Jaq ran over and grabbed him by the tail, pulling him back under the table, where he wouldn't be seen. Bonip tried to cling to his food, but it was too big for him.

"It's delicious," Bonip said, his face covered in crumbs.

Jaq's growling stomach overruled his cautious brain, and he sprinted out to grab the food stick. Back under the table, he pulled off a part of the edge and sniffed it. It was a little warm, and it smelled salty. He licked it with his tongue. It tasted round. Symmetrical curves of flavor floated into each other and caressed his mouth. He took a bite, and then another. He sighed loudly. Eating was such a delightful sensation.

Together they finished off the fluffy-crunchy-salty log. They looked around for more.

"Great Smolders, I was hungry," Jaq said.

Bonip found another log and moaned with pleasure as he ate.

But then the floor shook with tiny trembles, and a voice boomed above them. "Fiona!"

Jaq and Bonip hid behind the circular beam that held up the table. Jaq watched giant legs stride over to the entrance. He edged around the beam to keep his body out of sight. The giant pulled the glass door closed and locked it with a click.

Jaq looked at Bonip. "How are we going to get out?" he whispered.

Bonip, busy chewing, just shrugged.

"Fiona!" the giant bellowed again.

"I'm over here," a gentler, higher voice said from the back of the restaurant.

"Fiona, it's closing time. Quit reading and clean the tables," the giant said. "Then mop the floor and take out the garbage."

"Child labor laws, Uncle Gunther," Jaq heard the giant named Fiona mutter under her breath. "I'm only twelve."

"What did you say?" the bigger giant asked.

"Nothing." She walked over to the counter, where the bigger giant stood. Jaq, peeking around the table support, could see both giants now.

"Listen, if your mother is going to dump you on me after school, then you're gonna work—get it? I don't run a day-care center here."

"I know."

"You should be more grateful. Without me, you and your mom would be living on the street."

"Thank you, Uncle Gunther," Fiona said as the other giant handed her a spray bottle and a sponge. She walked right by Jaq and Bonip and muttered, "We're *so* grateful that you make us do all your chores, *and* charge us rent, *and* insult us every day."

Jaq watched as she squirted and cleaned table after table, starting at the far end and working her way toward the long counter in front of the cooking area. She wore an apron that held some salty sticks, and every now and then she'd reach in and eat one. Two white cords dangled from her ears, and she hummed along to some music playing very faintly.

"How are we going to get out of here, Bonip?" Jaq asked.

Bonip lay in a heap. "Don't know. Don't care. Feel sick."

Jaq felt panic rising inside him again. He looked from one

giant to the other, trying to figure out what to do. The girl giant was coming closer and closer. The other giant stood behind the long counter at the front of the restaurant, opening the metal boxes on top of the counter and pulling out green pieces of paper. Jaq felt exposed, with only the table support to duck behind. He looked around for another hiding place.

The room was filled with tables like the one he and Bonip were under, with some booths next to the far wall. A trash-collecting receptacle with plastic trays on top stood by the door. He might be able to hide behind it, but the giants would see him if he moved.

"Hey, Fiona," the man giant called. "Come here and look at this."

Jaq ducked behind the support post as Fiona walked by. The man giant, Jaq could see now, was taller and much stockier than Fiona, who was neat and slender. The man looked scruffy and powerful.

"Check this out. I got it for my girlfriend's kid at the toy shop upstairs." He held up a fat white bird. Only it wasn't a real bird. It was smooth and frozen, like a statue, but shiny. Jaq listened as the giant twisted something on the bottom of the animal and then set it on the counter. The bird started walking, its rigid legs making a spinning sound. And then it laid an egg. A bright blue egg.

The wonders of this planet!

The male giant thought it was hilarious.

The egg fell off the edge of the counter, bounced on the floor, and rolled toward Jaq and Bonip. Jaq's heart hammered in fear as the girl giant walked over to get the egg.

"Leave it. It's dirty now," the big giant said. The girl giant shrugged and turned back to the counter.

Jaq looked at the egg. It was so close. He could tell by its expensive and beautiful smell that it was something special. The giants weren't looking his way, so he tiptoed out and grabbed the egg.

"I knew it! It's glug," he whispered. "The bird laid a ball of glug. And it's fresh glug, too."

Bonip wasn't listening. He had eaten too much. He leaned away from Jaq and threw up.

Jaq stuffed the giant blue glugball into his backpack. He hoped the bird would lay another one.

A shrill ring sounded, making Jaq jump. Was it an alarm? Had he triggered something when he touched the valuable egg?

The ringing stopped, but after a few seconds it started

again, which distracted the man giant. He left the bird on the counter and turned toward the sound.

Jaq wondered if there were more birds like the glug–laying one on the counter. Imagine! Plenthy hadn't been lying when he called this a land of riches.

As Jaq was thinking, the giant Fiona reached for the bird and wound it up. The bird started walking again.

"Fiona, it's your mom," the other giant said. "Don't tell her you're working, okay?"

"But I *am* working."

The man giant came around the counter and grabbed Fiona by the arm. He yanked her, hard, his face boiling with anger. "I don't need any more of your back talk, Fiona. I swear, if you don't behave, I'll tell my dad that your mom is stealing from me and I'm kicking you guys out of my apartment."

"You wouldn't," Fiona said. "She's your sister."

"Stepsister. We're not blood. I'm doing my dad a favor letting you live with me. So you'll do what I tell you to do and not tell your mom. Got it?"

Fiona tried to pull her arm away, but that just made the bigger giant angry, and he squeezed harder. "Got it?" he repeated.

"Got it," Fiona answered. There was so much sadness in her voice that the sound swirled like dejected brown confetti before drifting to the ground. She left the bird and walked around the edge of the counter, disappearing from Jaq's sight. The man giant followed her.

The bird kept walking. It walked right off the counter and hit the floor.

Jaq didn't hesitate. He ran for the bird. It came up to his waist and was very heavy, but he dragged it back under the table where they'd been hiding.

Bonip had followed him out, but then he spotted another salty stick on the floor and sat down to eat it. *That stupid wipper!* Jaq cursed. He left the bird behind the post and ran out to grab Bonip, dragging him back toward the safety of the table support.

"What's this?" the man giant said. "Another rat! *Fiona!* Get the foam fumigator!"

"What?" Fiona called from behind the counter.

"I saw a rat scurry over there."

"I'm on the phone, Uncle Gunther."

"Just tell me where you left the fumigator—the foamy one. Hurry!"

"Hold on, I'm on the phone."

"Fiona! Find the foam fumigator!" the giant bellowed. "Hey, that's alliteration, you know."

Fiona appeared behind the counter. "I know what alliteration is, Uncle Gunther."

"Fiona, find the foam fumigator," Gunther repeated. "Fee-fi-fo-fum. HA!"

"You can't use that stuff again," Fiona said. "It leaves a stinky film over everything. It'll scare away the customers."

"So do rats!" Gunther shouted. "Where is it?"

"You put it on the high shelf, remember? I can't reach it."

"Fine." Gunther disappeared from Jaq's view.

Fiona came around the counter and got down on her hands and knees. She peered under tables and behind chairs. She was coming closer. Jaq pressed himself as flat as he could behind the pole, but she was going to find him. She would see the bright white bird and find him. He looked for a place to run, wondering if he could outrun a giant. Just as he was about to make a dash for the trash receptacle, a hand reached down and closed around him, squeezing him tight.

15

VICTORY IS A GIANT PLASTIC CHICKEN FILLED WITH GLUG

J AQ FELT HIMSELF RAISED UP, UP, UP IN THE air until he was face-to-face with the girl giant. She examined him with eyes that seemed as big as his head. Jaq was sure that she was going to eat him. "You're back! I knew you'd come back," she said. He felt himself turned around in her grasp. "Wait—you're not Plenthy."

"Eeep," Jaq squeaked.

"You're younger," she said. "And so skinny. Aww, you're just a kid."

"Eeep."

"FEE–FI–FO–FUM!" the man giant roared. "Fiona! I can't find it!" Jaq felt the ground rumble as the man giant searched behind the long counter. Metal smashed against metal. Jaq shook like the number 25, which is a very cowardly number.

Fiona looked at Jaq. "Where's Plenthy? I was beginning to think I'd just imagined him."

"Arp," Jaq said. "Urp."

"Hey, relax," Fiona said. "I won't hurt you. I'm just excited, I guess. When I told my mom I'd met a tiny little alien, she said I was making it up. Like I haven't heard *that* before. And then Plenthy disappeared, and I thought, *Maybe I* am *crazy.* But you're here now. I can show you to Mom, and then at least she'll know I was telling the truth."

Jaq's head shook no while his mouth said, "Nerp."

"You're shaking like a leaf."

"Home."

"You want to go home?"

Jaq nodded.

"Well, all right, little fella, I'll take you to your hidey-hole. Hey, you grabbed the plastic chicken. Do you want that?"

Jaq nodded.

"I don't care if you take it. My step-uncle Gunther is the worst." She wiped her eyes. "I hate him so much."

Jaq pointed to the half-eaten salty stick.

"You want some fries, too?"

Jaq nodded.

"Here, have some that haven't been on the floor."

Jaq held his backpack open, and Fiona filled it with fries. Then she scooped up the plastic bird. Jaq was relieved that she hadn't noticed Bonip clinging to the bird's legs. She unlocked the front door and walked out of the restaurant and across the open area, and placed Jaq on the edge of the indoor garden. "This is where Plenthy always went after exploring in the mall. Do you know him?"

Jaq shook his head. She was so big. Terrifyingly big. Even though she sounded nice, there was no getting around that bigness.

"You're still scared, aren't you?" Fiona asked.

Jaq nodded. She handed him the bird and smiled. "Don't worry. I won't let anything happen to you."

Jaq smiled.

Fiona smiled back. "What's your name?"

"Jaq," he said. "I'm Jaq."

"FIONA!" The man giant had spotted her. He was coming toward them.

"Go!" Fiona said. "But come back and visit again, okay?"

Jaq, still stunned, managed to say, "Maybe?"

"I'll keep an eye out for you. Be careful next time. Bye!"

Jaq rushed into the bushes and disappeared.

✳

Squish! Yank! Spin! They zipped through the wormhole and popped back out in the cave behind the waterfall. The glow from the wormhole faintly lit the space. Jaq stumbled forward, dropping the huge bird. What did she call it? A plastic chicken? He fell to his knees and kissed the ground.

"Home," he said. "We're home. And safe."

Bonip lay beside him, completely still.

"Are you okay, Bonip?" he asked.

Bonip nodded. His belly was hugely distended. "But I still feel sick."

Oh, the relief to be back on Yipsmix! Jaq's head immediately felt clear and sharp and focused. Unfortunately, the first thought that came to him was that he hadn't even tried to find that Plenthy fellow who needed help. He'd just grabbed the glug and left.

"That was really scary!" he said to Bonip, but he was really saying it to himself. It had been scary, and there wasn't anything more he could do—or was there? The girl giant knew Plenthy. She probably had a clue to his whereabouts.

Maybe Jaq should go back and ask her. He looked at Bonip, still unmoving. If the little wipper was injured, maybe Jaq should take him home. Yes, that was what he should do. He would take Bonip home and then think about going back for Plenthy.

"Hey, are you okay?"

Bonip burped. "So full. Arg."

"We have to get out of here," Jaq said. Just being next to the wormhole was making him nervous, like it might suck him back in. He glanced at it again. Was it dimmer than when he first went through? The electric shimmer of the wormhole seemed a bit less charged. "Can you lead me past the water-fall again?"

"I'll try. Just plop me on your shoulder."

They edged slowly out from behind the waterfall and down the path. Soon Jaq was able to walk with his eyes open and fingers in his ears, and then they were far enough away that he could pull them out.

"Bonip, I'm really glad you came with me," Jaq said. "I never would have gone through that wormhole if it weren't for you. And I would have jumped right back out of there, too. The things we saw! Can you believe it? A land of giants."

"This *here* is a land of giants," Bonip replied. "Dummy."

"You know, with all this glug, I'll be able to buy so much food for my mom and Grandpa. They're going to be so happy. I'll even buy you some worms, Bonip. A whole stinking bucket of worms."

"Don't talk about food," Bonip said, rubbing his belly.

"Giant pink wiggly worms." Jaq started walking down the path. "Squishy, melt-in-your-mouth worms. Meaty, juicy, delicious . . ."

Bonip moaned, then covered his ears.

It was a long walk home, and the day was almost over. The two moons rose over the hill as if they were glaring at the exhausted explorers. Jaq felt like they were the eyes of the sky god Smolders, judging him. *Look at you with your ill-gotten riches*, those eyes seemed to say, *while poor Plenthy is stuck somewhere on that loud and terrifying planet.*

At home, Jaq swung the gate open, and Bonip peeked out of the backpack. "Let me out here," he said. Jaq lowered him to the ground, and Bonip ran off into the fields without looking back.

Even after his long day, Jaq got home before his mother, who was working longer hours at the hushware factory, hoping to earn the money they needed for food, now that the fields were dead. She looked so tired when she walked through the door. She just plopped right down in her chair next to Grandpa, who was asleep, and closed her eyes. Jaq got her a footstool and took off her shoes.

"Mom?" he said. "I have something to show you. Remember that key I traded Klingdux for? Well, it had a secret note inside, and a map. I followed the map, and look what I found."

He pulled out the blue egg. It took two hands to hold it. His mother opened her eyes a crack—she was too tired to open them all the way—but when she saw what Jaq was holding, her eyes went wide.

"It's glug," Jaq said. "I'm sure it's glug. And there's more inside a giant bird I left outside."

Jaq's mom gasped. "Where did you find that?"

"Up by the waterfall." Jaq wasn't sure how much of the story he wanted to share with his mom, so he changed the subject. "Do you think we can sell it?"

His mother stood up and took the egg from Jaq. She held it carefully, turning it to examine every surface. Then she hugged it. "I can hardly believe it. It's fantastic. Oh, Jaq, this could save us!"

"I'll take it to the market tomorrow," Jaq said.

"This time take your grandfather," his mom said. "Make sure you get what it's worth."

They ate a happy dinner of cold crunchy sticks that Jaq had brought back in his backpack. They were slightly covered in wipper hair, but an empty stomach isn't picky.

16

BETRAYAL TASTES LIKE ROTTEN EGGS

THE NEXT MORNING, JAQ GOT UP EARLY TO walk to the river and get some worms. The river was farther away now, but Jaq didn't mind. He walked, imagining how surprised Bonip was going to be when he found the garden full of worms again. If there was one thing he knew about Bonip, it was that he was always hungry. Jaq smiled, picturing the gratitude on that little wipper's face.

Then he laughed out loud. *I can't believe it! Me, friends with a wipper!*

He filled his bucket with worms and walked home, ready

to place them in his small garden of brickleberries and vegetables. (Vegetables weren't so bad if you ate them while your mom read a nice story about minions or a funny poem.) While he walked, he happily dreamed of selling the glug and buying Klingdux back from Tormy Vilcot. Then he'd buy an irrigation system for the fields. After that, maybe he'd have enough left over to buy a fancy hoverbike. It would be amazing to show up at school in style. Kids would want to come over to his house just to ride with him, like they did with Tormy. He'd have lots of friends. It was going to be great.

If only he could get rid of that little nagging voice in the back of his brain that told him it wasn't going to be so great as long as Plenthy was still stuck on that sensory explosion called Earth. After all, it was Plenthy's note that had led Jaq to all this glug. He owed the guy, and he had to figure out how to rescue him.

"Well, well, well," a voice said. It came from the brickleberry bushes. "It's the skinny kid with the hair."

"Weren't you wearing that shirt yesterday?" another said.

"No, that was the scarecrow," another replied. "I have to say, the scarecrow wore it better."

"His clothes *are* awful," another said. "But they do take attention away from that nose."

Jaq recognized that last voice. "Bonip?" He looked over and saw a familiar twitchy nose duck back behind the rip-weed stalks.

"Bonip?" one of the wippers said. "You friends with this guy?"

"Friends? With him? Don't be ridiculous. He gets me worms, is all. Definitely not friends with that loser."

"Good, 'cause if you are friends with him, that means you gotta go. Talk about spoiling my flow."

"How about this one—you know why his clothes are torn? 'Cause even they can't wait to get away from him," Bonip suggested.

"Good one! Even his clothes don't want to hang out with him!"

The rest laughed and hurled more insults at Jaq.

"Yeah," Bonip continued. "He told me he's got seventeen senses . . . but I guess fashion sense ain't one of them!"

The wippers all roared with laughter.

Jaq felt crushed. He could withstand the other wippers' taunts. He'd put up strong mental walls to block those attacks, and the insults just bounced right off them. But Bonip had gotten past his defenses by being his friend. Or pretending to be. It's hard to steel yourself to an attack from inside your walls, because it's unexpected, which makes it hurt so much more. Jaq felt the betrayal through his whole body, from his shaky legs, to his gut, which felt like it had been punched, to his eyes, which blinked away tears as fast as they could form.

Sling you all! he wanted to shout. *I'm going to get my wipperslinger back, and I'm going to watch him hurl you, over and over. Throw you so hard, you hit that tree and never come back.*

He went inside, leaving his bucket of worms by the door.

It was midmorning by the time Grandpa was ready to go to the market. By then, Jaq's anger had gone back into hibernation. He focused on the good he was going to do with his glug and forgot about the wippers.

"Oh, my bones . . . Oh, my back . . . Oh, oh, oh," Grandpa said. "How long have we been walking?"

"We just left," Jaq said. "I literally just closed the gate behind us."

"Well, it seems like forever. Let me stop and take a rest." Grandpa leaned against the fence until it started to wobble. "There we go . . . Oh, oh, oh." He sat down on the ground. Every movement Grandpa made was accompanied by a grunt, which sent out small purple starbursts in Jaq's vision.

It was going to be a long walk to the marketplace. Jaq

looked up the road. How was he going to get Grandpa to walk all that way when he'd just collapsed after walking from the door to the gate, a total of twenty steps?

He had to get Grandpa moving.

"Grandpa," Jaq said, "tell me about how you lost the farm."

"I don't like to talk about it," Grandpa said, the anger inside him forcing him up to his feet. He started pacing. "It just makes me so mad."

Jaq hoped that an angry Grandpa would be a walking Grandpa, so he kept talking. "Were you swindled? Like me with the key?"

"Key? What key? I didn't even get a key out of the bargain, no," he said. "In that regard, you did me one better."

"What happened?" Jaq could remember visiting Grandpa at his old farm on just two occasions. It wasn't until Grandpa lost the farm sixteen years ago, when Jaq was only thirty-three, that Jaq and his mother had come to help take care of him. This little tract of land was all he had left by that time.

Grandpa stopped walking and turned to look at the Vilcots' enormous farm. Jaq watched his grandfather's gaze travel across the vineyard that separated their houses until it reached the Vilcots' home. Past the large house lay an open field filled with animals. It was a beautiful, bucolic landscape, but it reminded Grandpa of his loss.

Grandpa sighed. The sadness on his face was so raw and open that Jaq felt his insides get all jumbled up with sorrow.

He turned to Jaq. "I'm going to tell you what happened," he said, "even though I don't like talking about it. But if you can learn something from my mistake, then you should hear it."

He leaned against the fence and continued. "Many years ago, I was enjoying life on my magnificent farm, happy as a 16 that doesn't know a square root is sneaking up, ready to demolish him into a 4. Did I tell you about the manzeeno orchard down by the river?"

"Yes, Grandpa. Let's focus on the swindle."

"Right. I'll start over . . . There I was, not a rumble of sadness in my whole being, when who should come for a visit but an old school chum. He'd just moved back to town after living a life of adventure. Oh! The stories he could tell! They were filled with delicious and exotic words, like *chimichanga* and *escalator* and *jambalaya*.

"Well, my old pal had a fantastic new enterprise that was going to bring unbelievable riches to our world. He just needed some cash to get it going. I had a nice farm, as I've told you. Did I mention the wild guarthaberry bushes?"

"Yes. Did you give him money?"

"Well, here's the situation. I had this nice farm, as you know—"

"I know," Jaq said, before Grandpa could start reminiscing again.

"But not a lot of cash. You know farming, Jaq. The money is tied up in the crops and livestock. I had some available funds, but not enough. So I asked my friend Ripley Vilcot to invest with us. We'd each own a third of the business."

"Your *friend* Vilcot?" Jaq said.

"Yep, we were friends once," Grandpa said. He shook his head, as if even he couldn't believe it. At last, he started walking again. "That is, until this other fellow disappeared with our money and Vilcot accused me of being part of the swindle. Vilcot is a prideful man, and he wanted his money back. A Rollop always pays his debts, Jaq. I've told you that before, haven't I?"

"Yes, Grandpa."

"I had to sell my farm to pay back every last damar he'd invested. It wasn't enough for Vilcot, though. He wanted to punish me for tricking him, but the police said they couldn't arrest me, because I'd given him his money back. This infuriated Vilcot, so he bought my farm from the fella I'd sold it to and has been making my life miserable ever since. I can't get a job because he tells everyone I'm a crook."

"But can't he see you weren't part of the swindle?" Jaq asked. "If you were, you'd have more money."

"He thinks I set him up and then got swindled out of my share." Grandpa stopped walking again. They had passed the vineyards and now stood in front of the Vilcots' house. "I curse the day that my old friend came back to town. He stole everything from me—my farm, my money, and my trust in people. A thief always steals more than he knows. Oh, he may think he's just taking your money, but he's also leaving behind a minefield of sadness. Little explosions of despair pierce your heart whenever you think about what you lost. You never know when those sad memories of loss will strike, and they never go away. That's what a thief does—leaves behind a lot of sorrow. I couldn't live with myself if I knew how much sadness I was causing."

The man sounded an awful lot like the Swindler, and Jaq knew exactly where to find him: shopping at the marketplace with the money he'd gotten from selling Klingdux. Jaq would tell Grandpa about him as soon as they were done selling the glug. He needed to keep Grandpa focused.

Jaq's stare-sense drew his attention to a window in the

Vilcots' house, where he saw Ripley Vilcot scowling down at them.

"Let's get moving," Jaq said.

Grandpa nodded, and they set off down the road for the market.

17

PRIDE IS PARANOID,
LIKE AN ORANGE 6

OLD RIPLEY VILCOT WAS EXPECTING A visitor.

He stood at the wide window while his grandson, Tormy, sat on the floor next to him throwing a ball to Klingdux. Vilcot had wanted the boy with him for this meeting. Tormy needed to learn how to deal with shifty people.

Vilcot didn't like waiting. He also didn't like what he saw outside—that devious old Rollop and his grandson. They were just standing there, looking at his farm. Oh, how he hated that family. What were they up to with that big plastic bird? Vilcot didn't like it. He didn't like it one bit. As he scowled at the pair of them, the boy looked up and saw him. Then they hurried away, looking guilty.

Vilcot's thoughts were interrupted by a knock on the door.

"Pay attention, Tormy," he said. "But first, let him in."

Tormy opened the door, then returned to his spot on the floor with Klingdux.

Vilcot remained standing, gazing out the window. He wanted his visitor to squirm a little, to get nervous about why he'd been called into his boss's office. This was not a day to mess with Ripley Vilcot.

At last, the elder Vilcot turned around and spoke. No greeting, no explanation, he got right to business. "How much did you give that boy for this freasel, hmm?" He pointed to Klingdux.

"What did we agree on?" Davardi replied. "You said no more than thirty. Those were the instructions I followed."

"I'm well aware of what I told you. I did not ask you what my instructions were. I asked you how much you gave the boy. And the reason I am asking, Mr. Davardi, is that this morning, my colleague at the hushware factory told me that Mrs. Rollop was happier than a 3. She's been telling her friends that her money problems are over. I'm asking because you're standing before me in an expensive leather jacket and matching boots that you weren't wearing when I gave you the money."

"I happen to own lots of clothes that you haven't seen, Vilcot."

"Ah, but do you leave the tags on all of them?"

Davardi spun around in circles until he found the offending tag, then plucked it off and stuffed it into a pocket.

Ripley Vilcot came out from behind his desk and approached Davardi, giving him a long, slow gaze from his face down to his new boots and back again. *The man is devious*, he thought. *I knew I shouldn't have trusted him.* Small curlicues of black and deep red spun in the corners of his vision.

"I know how to add things up, Davardi, and this doesn't add up. I know you're as shifty as an 8, so tell me now what you gave that boy, or I will make your life miserable. Don't think I can't."

Davardi shuffled his feet and looked at the floor. "I didn't give him any damars. I kept them for myself and bought this jacket. I traded for the freasel."

"Traded what?"

"That big key you gave me. It's pretty, but worthless. It doesn't open anything."

"That kid traded his pet for a key?" Vilcot had trouble believing Davardi's explanation.

"The key and a story." Davardi smiled. "I've got a way with words, if I do say so myself."

Vilcot nodded. He dismissed Davardi with a swish of his hand. He believed Davardi was telling the truth, but it still didn't add up. How could a key make the Rollops so happy?

That key! Oh, how Vilcot hated that key! He'd been happy to get rid of it. But now here it was again, popping up in a situation that had already made him angry.

Whenever he thought about the key, Vilcot's jaw clenched in anger. It reminded him of the time he'd lost all his money to Rollop and his con man friend, Plenthy. Sure, he'd gotten his money back from that wicked Rollop, but the thought that he'd been conned still stung his pride. And the key was a slap in the face, meant to remind him of his stupidity.

Years after Plenthy had disappeared, a messenger had come to the farm and said, "Plenthy told me to give this to you." At first, Vilcot thought it might be a letter of apology, along with a check reimbursing him for his investment, plus interest. But, no, it was just a key. Nothing else. No note, no money, no apology. Just a stupid, old-fashioned key.

To Vilcot, it was a cruel gesture on Plenthy's part. It was

as if he was saying, *I've got your money. Here, have this worthless key. Sucker.*

At first, Vilcot put the key on a stand and kept it on his desk to remind him that people, even friends, were always trying to take advantage. Always. You couldn't trust anyone. He'd sit at his desk, negotiating deals with other people, and then he'd look at the key and negotiate even harder. He was merciless and never gave an inch. Sometimes the other party got up and left, but no matter! They recognized they wouldn't be able to swindle old Ripley Vilcot and probably went on to easier targets.

That reminded him that he still needed to find someone to tend his winnowberry vines, which were dying. Nobody seemed to want to work for him. Bunch of swindlers.

Vilcot shook his head. *Forget about the vines.*

He began to pace as he thought, but as soon as he started walking, he stumbled over Klingdux, who yipped in pain. Vilcot kicked the pest out of the way, and Klingdux yipped again before huddling against the wall. Tormy threw the ball at Klingdux to punish him for not getting out of the way. Then he laughed.

Vilcot nodded in approval. Then his thoughts returned to the key. He'd gotten so tired of looking at that key and being reminded of his stupidity that he'd given it to Davardi. It looked expensive, so Davardi had immediately wanted it. Foolish, superficial man. And once he realized it was worthless, he'd given it to the Rollops in exchange for that freasel.

But that didn't explain why Mrs. Rollop was so happy. If Davardi hadn't paid for the freasel, then how had Mrs. Rollop suddenly come into money? Why was that boy dragging around a giant fake bird? What were those Rollops up to?

There could be only one answer. Old Rollop must have found that swindler Plenthy. Old Rollop had gotten his money back . . . he'd gotten *Vilcot's* money back.

Vilcot wanted his money back. Even though he'd taken more from Rollop than he'd lost in his investment, he wanted *his* money back. It was money he'd been tricked out of, and he was a man who couldn't stand being tricked.

He began to form a plan. Swishes of color swirled in his mind as he imagined himself arguing with people. He loved confrontations. They made him feel powerful. Arguing was like taking those pulsing swirls of red and black and hurling them at other people. He never tired of the thrill of binding other people up with his angry swirls of color.

"Tormy," he said, "what happened to the giant bird I

bought for you after you got a one hundred percent on your homework?"

"You never—"

"I do believe that Rollop boy stole it from you, didn't he?"

"But, Grandfather, you never gave me a—"

"I did. And Jaq stole it from you. How else could a poor, pathetic kid like that have something so grand?"

"Oh, I get it. Yeah. That was my bird. And he stole it. 'Cause he was mad I bought his wipper–slinger."

"Exactly. We should call the police."

18

FOR THE UNSUSPECTING, DANGER WAITS

J AQ AND HIS GRANDPA CONTINUED THEIR slow walk, each lost in his own thoughts. Past the Vilcots' spread they continued down the dusty road, nearing the market.

"I wish I could find that old Plenthy," Grandpa said. "I'd drag him back here and make him tell Vilcot the truth."

Jaq blinked a few times, unsure that the taste in his mouth was really what he had just heard. "Did you say 'Plenthy'?"

"Yes, that was my friend's name," Grandpa said. "Yorlim Plenthy."

"Grandpa, I know where Plenthy is. He's on Earth."

"Where's Earth?"

"Plenthy wrote the note in the key!" Jaq said.

"What key?" Grandpa asked. "The one you got for your pet? Hey, I never got a look at that key. You still have it?"

Jaq opened his backpack and pulled out the key.

"Hot tamale!" Grandpa said. "That's from Plenthy, all right."

"I told you that," Jaq said. "Are you saying that your partner . . . was Plenthy? That he's the guy who took your money and ran? That it wasn't Davardi?"

"Davardi? That dandy fellow who hangs out in the market? Good grief, no. And if you ask me, Davardi is not that man's real name."

"How do you know about the key?"

"Because it's mine!" Grandpa spun the key around in his hand. "It's a funny gizmo I picked up at the fair. I was waiting in line, a line that got longer when the Vilcots cut in, and a lady came by selling these. They open up, so you can stick a note inside. You can give it to your girlfriend and tell her it's the key to your heart. Or give it to a friend and call it the key to happiness. It's just a fun novelty.

"Anyway, after we made our deal, I gave it to Plenthy with

a note inside that said, 'It's our key to success!' Ha! What a fool I was."

"How did Davardi get it?" Jaq asked.

"Hmm . . . I have no idea. What did the note inside say?"

Jaq showed him the note.

"This was meant for me," Grandpa said. "Jaq, you numb-skull—you do know my name is Greggin, don't you? It's not 'Grandpa.'"

"It's such a common name, I didn't put it together," Jaq said. "Plus, it says only someone with 'your resources and unwavering courage' could help him."

"What are you saying?"

"Um. That you don't have either."

"Well, not anymore, I'll grant you," Grandpa said, waving a finger in the air. "But back in the day I would have fought as hard as Klingdux for a worthy cause—"

"Why would Davardi have a key with a note for you? It doesn't make sense."

"I wonder . . . ," Grandpa said. "Let's see. This is what we know: You got this key from Davardi, who was working for Vilcot when he stole Klingdux. He probably got the key from Vilcot. But how did Vilcot get it? Hmm. If Plenthy wanted to send me a note, he'd send it to my old farm. Wait! That's it! Plenthy didn't know that I'd sold it." Grandpa pointed back toward the Vilcots' farm. "So Plenthy's messenger gave this key to Vilcot, thinking that Vilcot was me. Vilcot never opened it, because he doesn't know the secret."

"Is the secret having your mother throw it out the window?"

"Ha-ha, no. There's a twist here, and then you push this prong. Presto." The key split apart, revealing the hollow tube in the shaft. Grandpa twirled the pieces in his hands. "Well, he's got some nerve, doesn't he?"

"What do you mean?"

"Plenthy took my money, he took Vilcot's money, and then he disappeared. Not a word for years. And now that he's in trouble, he asks for help. Promising me riches! Ha! I've heard *that* before."

"Grandpa, this bird and the glug inside it are from Earth."

Grandpa looked down at the bird. "Is that so?"

"Yes. But Earth is scary," Jaq said. "It's filled with giants. And the place is a sensory explosion of the worst kind. So many sounds, smells, tastes, sights, and feels. Everything is so loud and bright and harsh. It's crazy."

"But you went before," Grandpa said. "If you did it once, we can do it again. You and I together—we can go back and find Plenthy. I'd love to see Vilcot's face when Plenthy tells him I didn't steal his money. That's all I want out of that old swindler! We have to go."

Jaq kicked a rock and hurt his toe. "I know," he said. "When I think of being trapped there, it's awful. Nobody deserves that. We should rescue him. I did meet one nice giant. Her name is Fiona, and she seemed to know Plenthy. She might be able to help."

"All right, then," Grandpa said. "We'll sell this glug, buy a few rescue supplies, and then go save Plenthy. Who knows? Maybe we'll find more glug. Enough to buy my farm back."

Jaq smiled. Grandpa seemed to have filled up with energy. This was fantastic. The two of them could rescue Plenthy together. It would be great to have Grandpa with him. Jaq knew he would feel a lot less scared.

They walked down the road, faster now, their steps buoyed with excitement. If this plan worked, their problems would be over.

And then Jaq noticed a group of hoverbikes heading their way.

They were police hoverbikes.

Jaq and his grandfather stood aside to let the police officers pass, but the hoverbikes surrounded them. Jaq looked from one stern face to another. Something was very wrong here. Jaq felt his heart beat hard and fast, like it was trying to warn him.

"Put the bird down, young man," the officer in front said. The rest dismounted.

More hoverbikes approached from the other direction. Jaq saw Tormy Vilcot and his grandfather racing right for them, followed by two of their ranch hands.

"There he is! And that's my bird!" Tormy shouted. He and his grandfather looked angrier than an 84.

Jaq turned to Grandpa, who was shaking his head.

Once the Vilcots reached the group, Ripley Vilcot dismounted and charged right at Grandpa. "This is because of the farm, isn't it?" he said. "You two see us with anything, and you have to try to steal it."

"That's not true," Jaq said. "My grandfather never stole anything in his life."

"Your grandfather has been caught stealing fruit from Mr. Vilcot's orchard multiple times," the policeman said. "Mr. Vilcot kindly hasn't pressed charges, but this is a different thing entirely. Stealing from a little kid."

"*I'm* a little kid," Jaq said. "And I didn't steal this. It was a gift."

"From whom?" Ripley Vilcot asked. His greedy eyes bored right into Jaq, just begging him to keep talking.

Jaq looked to Grandpa, wondering if he should say anything. If he told them about the wormhole and Earth, then the greedy Vilcots would go there and steal all the glug for themselves.

"Listen," Vilcot said. "I can see what's up, Greggin. You've found Plenthy. You've gotten your money back. Well, I want my money back, too. Tell me where he is, and I'll let this go."

"Let this go?" Grandpa said. "*Let this go?* You must be joking. You're not owed anything, you greedy old coot! I paid you back in full."

What happened next was a blur to Jaq. Grandpa lunged at Vilcot, his rage overtaking him completely. Jaq had never seen Grandpa move so quickly. While Jaq stood watching in shock, Tormy tackled him from behind and pinned him to the ground. The policemen were busy trying to break up the grandfathers, so Tormy got in a few punches to Jaq's ribs before anyone noticed.

Once Tormy was off him, Jaq rolled to his side and moaned.

"It's my bird," Tormy said. He grabbed it and handed it to one of the ranch hands. Then he noticed Jaq's backpack.

"What else of mine have you taken?" Tormy opened the pack and pulled out the blue glug egg. "Also mine," he said, smirking.

"Take him away," the elder Vilcot said. He was pointing to Grandpa. Vilcot's hair was mussed up, and he smoothed it down with his gloved hands. "Lock him up for stealing and assault. And then go arrest the boy's mother. She was an accomplice."

"No!" Jaq said. If they arrested his mother, she'd lose her job. Then they'd be worse off than ever.

Jaq's grandpa kept swinging at Vilcot, so the policemen cuffed his hands and shoved him into the criminal trailer, which was a small cell attached to one of the hoverbikes. Grandpa kept swearing at the policemen and Vilcot until the door was closed and the sound cut off.

"I'm a compassionate man, Roamy," Vilcot said to one of the policemen. "You know me. I don't want this poor, misguided boy to be left alone, and I'm satisfied with the return of our property. As long as the boy apologizes for stealing, we won't press charges against his mother."

The policemen looked at Ripley Vilcot as if he were the nicest guy they'd ever met. It made Jaq want to vomit.

He didn't know what to do. He hated the Vilcots. Why did

they think they could just take whatever they wanted? The chicken was Jaq's dream of a better life for his mother and grandfather, and now selfish Tormy Vilcot had snatched it from his grasp. Jaq knew he should fight them, but if he did, they'd just take the chicken anyway and his mother would lose her job. He had no way to prove it was his.

"I'm sorry for stealing it," Jaq said.

Tormy leaned in close and whispered in Jaq's ear. "You don't even put up a fight, do you? You're such a coward."

The Vilcots took their loot, got back on their hoverbikes, and headed home. The policemen also drove off, in the opposite direction, with Jaq's grandpa. Jaq ran after them, screaming, "He didn't do anything!"

But soon they were out of reach.

19

FORGIVENESS IS
A SUPERPOWER

JAQ SAT AT HOME, WONDERING WHAT TO DO. He had to save his grandfather, and he knew the only way to do that was to rescue Plenthy and bring him back to Yipsmix. That meant going back to Earth, a prospect that terrified him.

How could he go back to Earth alone? The giants were so big, and the planet was so overwhelming.

As he sat there hunting for some courage, his mother came home.

"Jaq," she said, "I just got back from town. They won't

release Grandpa." She dropped her bag and paced. "I told them he's not going anywhere, but they want to keep him in jail until the judges can rule on his case. That could take forever! And what if they find him guilty? What are we going to do?"

"They stole my chicken," Jaq said. "Those Vilcots. They told the police that I'd taken it from Tormy. And the police believed them."

"Of course they did. Ripley Vilcot has bribed everyone in town. Grandpa is never going to be free." Mom shook her head. "I have to get back to work. I'll be home late, to make up for the time I took off this afternoon. Will you be okay?"

Jaq nodded. After a pause, he said, "What if I could get another one? Another glug-filled bird."

Mom stopped pacing and looked at him. "How?"

"It's a long story," Jaq said. "But to do it, I need to ask you a question."

"What?"

"When you're working at the factory, how do you handle all the noise? Doesn't it fill your mouth with flavors and your vision with colors and shapes? Doesn't it make it impossible to fuction?"

She opened her bag. "They give us these," she said, pulling out a package of earplugs and some thick earmuffs. "And this," she said, holding up a nose plug on a rubbery string. "And sometimes I wear these," she said, putting on a pair of sunglasses. "And this." She shook out a package of Blandie Biscuits—The Biscuit That Fights Off Flavor. "Eat one of those, and no unpleasant tastes will pop into your mouth unexpectedly."

"To get another bird, I have to go up by the waterfall," Jaq said. "It's really hard to walk next to it."

Mom nodded. "Take them," she said. "And, Jaq"—she grabbed his shoulders and looked him in the eye—"tell me that the waterfall is the only danger. Promise me. I could not bear it if anything happened to you."

"I promise," Jaq said. "I'll be fine."

It was the hardest lie Jaq had ever told.

✳

The Vilcots may think that they've won. But I'm going to show them. I'm not done fighting.

Jaq knew that's what Klingdux the superhero would say in this situation, but Jaq was having trouble finding the same resolve.

Easy for him to say, Jaq thought. *Klingdux is an indestructible superhero. It's much harder to be brave when you are small and very, very destructible.*

Jaq knew that if he had superstrength or speed or a magical suit, he probably wouldn't be afraid of anything, either. But he didn't, so he was. Still, he had to go back. If there was even the smallest chance that he could save his family by bringing Plenthy back to testify for Grandpa, or by bringing home more glug, he had to try.

He raced past the Vilcuts' farm, not wanting to see a single member of that evil family. He slowed to a walk once he'd passed it. That was when he noticed the pack shift on his back. He stopped and opened it up. Inside he saw the earplugs, earmuffs, sunglasses, nose plug, the Blandie Bisquits, the key, the map, and a furry nose.

"I'm hungry," Bonip said.

"Bonip! What are you doing in there?"

"I was looking for some crispy-stick crumbs. And before I know it, you've dropped these earmuffs on my head and we're bouncing along. I'm still hungry. Did I mention that?"

"Yes, you did," Jaq said. He dumped his backpack upside down, catching his earmuffs but letting Bonip fall to the ground.

"Hey!"

"Go on." Jaq pointed. "Go back to your friends. I'd rather be alone than with a traitor like you."

"Come on, Mr. Seventeen Senses, don't you have a sense of humor?" Bonip asked. When he started laughing, Jaq pulled his leg back to kick the rotten little rodent.

"No, really. I'm truly, truly sorry," Bonip said, serious now. "I'm sorry I teased you. It's just . . . they make me feel so . . . so . . . like if I don't join them, then I must be the biggest loser, you know? I'm really sorry."

Jaq scowled at him.

"Let me come. I can help," Bonip said. "I'll get you past the waterfall."

Jaq showed Bonip his earmuffs.

"I'll look right when you look left. Okay?"

Jaq sighed. As much as he hated wippers, and especially this little traitorous one, he had to admit that he felt a little less afraid when he had someone with him. "All right, you can come. But you have to promise to listen to me. And if we do get to Earth, you can't have any crunchy sticks until I say so. We have to find Fiona and then find Plenthy. Then we eat. Got it?"

"I promise."

"Okay, hop in." Jaq held open the backpack. Bonip jumped in, and Jaq put it back on.

Bonip peeked out the top. "Did I mention I was hungry?"

Among his seventeen senses, Jaq had a terrific sense of direction, and he found his way straight back to the wormhole. He came prepared this time, wearing both earplugs and earmuffs as he approached the waterfall. The muffled roar was no more than a faint echo of color in his vision, and he navigated through it easily.

He approached the swirly gateway and put up his hands, like before. Then he pulled off his earmuffs. He had to make sure Bonip understood the plan.

"Bonip, here we go. Remember, we have to find that nice girl giant. She can tell us what she knows about Plenthy. Then we'll find food."

"I know, I know. Let's get going."

Jaq resecured the earmuffs. He put on the nose plug and the sunglasses. He popped a biscuit into his mouth. He nodded at Bonip and stepped through. This time he felt a little more squished, a little more tugged, and his breath was sucked out of him a little faster. Then he was in the soil again, and he took in a big breath of air.

"That was so much worse than the first time," he said. "Hey, does the wormhole look fainter to you?"

It looked like Bonip agreed—he was nodding and talking, but Jaq couldn't hear him because of the earmuffs.

Jaq stood and regained his sense of balance. With his other senses muted, he was able to concentrate on closing off the connections in his flexible brain. He breathed deeply and removed his protection one by one: first the earmuffs, then the earplugs, then the sunglasses, and, finally, the nose plug. As much as he wanted to keep them on, he knew that he'd need his senses to survive on Earth.

Poor Earthlings. They had to filter out so much unnecessary information every second. If there was one thing Jaq had noticed about this alien world, it was that Earth was filled with unnecessary information, all of it fighting for attention: sounds crashing into brightly colored signs, smells charging through a confusion of tastes, hums and clicks and odors and chatter. It took some time to mentally mute it all, but at last Jaq felt stable and in control.

"Let's go find some food," Bonip said.

"Bonip, I told you—we have to find Fiona. But I have to hide my stuff first." Jaq made a pile of his gear and put his empty backpack back on. He planned to fill it with glug. The soil was soft, so he started digging a hole. "Why don't you look out for Fiona while I hide everything?" he said.

"Okay, but hurry." Bonip hopped over to the edge of the plants. "Oooh, there's some sort of show going on. There's a small crowd of giants watching a guy on a stage. He's dressed in black and waving a long stick in the air . . . *Snorks!* The stick just turned into a bunch of flowers. Ha!"

Jaq was rethinking his hiding place. He didn't want his mom's stuff to be smothered in dirt. He looked around for a leaf to cover them with, but all the leaves were still clinging tightly to plants. "Any sign of Fiona?" he asked.

"No. I want to watch this guy. Now he's got a long rope . . . He's folding it in half . . . He's cutting the rope . . . What's he going to do now, I wonder?"

"If you're not going to look for Fiona, you could help me rip off this leaf. It might go a little faster. I know you have sharp teeth."

"Worm cakes! He's made the rope whole again! Like magic."

There was some unenthusiastic applause. The audience clearly wasn't as impressed with the performance as Bonip was.

A new song drifted out of the loudspeakers flanking the stage.

"This is going to be good, I can tell," Bonip said. "Okay, now he's bringing out a giant glass cage."

Something besides the annoying voice of the wipper

caught Jaq's ear. "Be quiet for a second," he said. "I want to listen to that song."

"I tell you, that's a tough crowd. They're barely even clapping. Some of those giants are walking away, shaking their heads."

"Shh!"

"All right, all right. *Sorry.*"

The song was unlike anything Jaq had ever heard, and he stopped pulling at the leaf to listen. It filled his brain with such vivid pictures and sensations. He found that he was holding his breath to the very end, when the music built up to a crescendo and made him cover his ears.

Wow! he thought when it was over.

The memory of the song echoed in his brain, like a slide show of sensations.

A deep voice boomed through the air. "And now, ladies and gentlemen . . . for my final act, I, Morgo the Magnificent, will perform a trick never before seen by human eyes." His voice was so loud, it seemed to echo off the walls. "Behold, the Incredible Shrinking Magician!"

Jaq edged next to Bonip and watched the giant approach the tall glass case. The song started again, the same one, and Jaq saw and felt the same sensations as before. It was almost like he was being lifted up, then the air filled with popping colors, and then, as the music went on, each sensation was replaced by a new one. Normally when he listened to music, he saw random swishes of color, while air seemed to brush against his skin, but this was different. He wanted to hear it again, and again, and again.

The magician had slicked-back black hair, a mask over his eyes, and a cape. He exaggerated every movement with elaborate gestures and meaningful looks at the audience. He stepped into the tank and closed it, running his hands all around the inside to show it was secure.

"He's really hamming it up, I have to say," Bonip said.

Morgo the Magnificent pulled a cord, and a red curtain covered the tank. Fog billowed out from the bottom and waterfalled off the edge of the stage. The curtain rose back up, revealing an empty tank.

No—it wasn't empty.

"Oh! That's fantastic!" Bonip said. "He's little now. He's doing that wand trick again, with the flowers, but he's smaller."

A tiny magician stood in the tank, waved the flowers at the crowd, and bowed. The crowd edged closer, oohing and aahing.

"Spicy worms, that was amazing!" Bonip said.

"Bonip!" Jaq said. "Look at him."

Bonip looked at Jaq. He looked back at the stage, where the little magician in the glass tank was doing another trick. He looked back at Jaq. He gasped. "Jaq, are you thinking what I'm thinking?"

"Yes, I am," Jaq said.

"These giants can change size at will!"

"No, you idiot!" Jaq said. "The little man is Plenthy! You know, the guy who wrote the note asking for help. We have to save him."

20

I FEEL A SONG IN MY HEART, AND ALSO ON MY ARMS, AND A LITTLE ON MY CHEEK

J AQ AND BONIP RACED THROUGII THE plants that bordered the side of the big open space until they were as close to the stage as they could get while still staying safely hidden. Jaq was certain that the little man in the tank was a Yipsmixer. He was doing the rope trick now, looking at the crowd as his little hands held a smaller rope up high.

Jaq peeked out and waved, trying to get his attention.

The little magician folded the rope in his hands and cut

the loop. He did the moves robotically, completely uninter-
ested in his own trick. He looked up again.

Jaq waved like mad. *If he sees me*, he thought, *then maybe he
can give me a clue as to how to rescue him.*

He waved furiously.

And Plenthy's bored eyes suddenly lit up.

"He's mouthing something," Bonip said from his perch on
Jaq's shoulder. "Can you tell?"

"It looks like he's saying *magic*," Jaq said. He edged closer.
"No, it's *music*."

"Wait," Bonip said. "Now he's saying, *Look out!*"

A giant hand suddenly appeared from nowhere, curved
around Jaq's middle, and lifted him out of the bushes. Bonip
fell off his shoulder. Jaq felt a scream ready to burst from his
lungs, but he clamped down on it, terrified.

"Got you."

Jaq found himself face-to-face with the giant called Uncle
Gunther. The fearsome creature smiled, revealing teeth that
were speckled with food. His breath was horrible. Jaq felt
like he was being bathed in a burp.

"You're not getting away this time," the giant said, smiling. "In fact, you're gonna make me some money. Morgo will
pay big for another little guy like you."

Jaq struggled in the grip of the huge monster. His mind filled with the terrifying image of being stuck in a glass box like Plenthy. He squirmed and twisted, but it was no use. Gunther had stuffed him beneath his jacket and was holding him tight. Jaq sensed that the giant was walking quickly, and that he was getting farther and farther away from the safety of the wormhole.

Suddenly, the giant stopped walking and shook his leg. He reached down to scratch his ankle, then his calf, and then the back of his knee. And then he scratched all those places faster and more frantically. Jaq was pulled out from the jacket, and Gunther switched him from hand to hand, trying to get at the itch.

"Ouch," Gunther said. "Ow! Ouch! What the—?"

He reached behind him with his free hand, trying to scratch a spot on his back.

Jaq was swirled about in the air. Up and down, left and right, the grip tightening and loosening as Gunther did his strange dance. Gunther jumped behind a pillar to avoid the stares of the other giants.

"Ouch. Dagnabbit!"

Oh, Bonip—you amazing little wipper, Jaq thought.

"Uncle Gunther, what's wrong?" It was Fiona's voice.

Jaq looked over and saw her just before Gunther swung him around and blocked her from his view.

"Something's biting me. Ouch! It's driving me crazy!" He switched Jaq to his other hand, and when he did, Jaq bit down hard. Gunther flung Jaq away, and he sailed through the air, hitting a pillar and then falling into a planter. He thumped into soft soil.

"Let me look," Fiona said.

"It stings!" Gunther cried. "I feel burns all up and down my back. And it's still biting! Get it off me!"

"Fiona! Help!" Jaq cried from the planter.

Gunther was too frantic from the biting to hear Jaq, but Fiona heard him. She looked right at him, and he waved his hands.

"You should go to the bathroom and take off your shirt," Fiona told her uncle. "Splash some water on your back or something."

Gunther nodded. Jaq saw Bonip crawl out of the top of the giant's shirt. The little wipper jumped unseen from Gunther's back to Fiona's shoulder just as Fiona reached down and grabbed Jaq. She sprinted away, hiding Jaq from Gunther.

"Fiona!" Gunther yelled, still scratching.

"Be right back!" Fiona yelled. "Go to the bathroom!"

"Come back! I need your help!"

Fiona ran to a moving staircase in the middle of the mall, and they were lifted to safety.

As he bounced along beneath Fiona's jacket, Jaq felt sick. He knew they were heading away from the wormhole, and with each step, his panic intensified. The magic show must have ended because the giants who had been watching now filled the hallways of the mall. Jaq could see through a button-hole in Fiona's jacket that there were huge bodies every-where.

At last, Fiona ducked into a restaurant and ran to a booth in the back. She sat down, placing Jaq on a vinyl bench that stretched under a table. Her focus stayed on the door.

"Is he coming?" Jaq asked.

"No," Fiona said. "I think we're safe. *Phew.*"

"Thanks for saving me." Jaq sat down on the rubbery seat, fatigue replacing the fear he'd been feeling. "You too, Bonip."

"Who's Bonip?" Fiona asked.

"Him." Jaq pointed to her shoulder

Fiona nearly flicked the little fluffball off her shoulder, but she froze when Bonip waved at her.

"Oh my goodness," Fiona said. "He's so small, like a fluffy white roly-poly bug."

"He's a wipper," Jaq said. "Your uncle Gunther's sense of itch was going crazy, thanks to this guy. I've never seen anyone react to a wipper bite like that. He must be really sensitive to the poison. Good job, Bonip."

"Just doing what comes naturally," Bonip said modestly. He jumped off Fiona's shoulder and landed next to Jaq. He spat a couple of times and then wiped his mouth. "Ew, that guy was so hairy."

"Hey," Jaq said, realizing something. "All those times you didn't even break my skin—you weren't really trying, were you?"

"You taste funny," Bonip said.

Jaq smiled. He looked up at Fiona. "Where are we?" he asked.

"This is a Mexican restaurant," Fiona said.

Jaq risked a peek by pulling himself up to look over the top of the table. The restaurant was mostly empty, but a couple of giants stood next to a long counter, looking through a glass shield at what lay underneath. They were selecting different items from tilted containers and adding them to their plates.

"Food?" Bonip asked, following Jaq's gaze.

"That's the salad bar," Fiona answered, but Bonip had already bounced over to it. She turned to Jaq. "This is the quietest restaurant in the mall, which is why Plenthy and I like it."

"You and Plenthy are friends?" Jaq asked.

"Yes. He got caught in a humane rat trap, and I rescued him. We've been friends ever since. I have something called synesthesia, and he's the only person I've met who understands. He believed me when I told him that I can see sounds."

"Can't everyone?" Jaq asked.

"No. Very few people on Earth have synesthesia, and no two people seem to have the same type. Usually, if I tell people that their whistling makes me see green lines, they look at me like I'm crazy." Fiona sighed. "Nobody I know senses things like I do."

"Like what?"

"That 4s are purple," Fiona said, pointing to the number on the menu. "That when I do this"—she tapped her finger on the table—"I see little brown flashing dots."

"Me too."

"That's what Plenthy said!" Fiona laughed. "Oh, he's the best. He told me not to tell anyone about him, and I laughed, because of course I wouldn't. If people thought I was crazy for seeing colors that aren't there, they'd probably lock me up if I told them I was friends with a little alien."

"Morgo the Magnificent has him now," Jaq said. "We saw him. That's how I got grabbed by your uncle."

"Wait . . . you *saw* Plenthy?"

"Yes, he was in that magic show downstairs."

"I thought he'd abandoned me. I have to talk to him," Fiona said, looking panicky herself now. "I *really* have to talk to him. He's the only one who can save me." She reached over and grabbed Jaq and raced out the door, holding him beneath her jacket again.

"Bonip!" Jaq yelled, but his voice was muffled. The wipper wouldn't have heard him anyway—his head was happily submerged in the shredded-cheese container.

21

ONE MAN'S TRASH IS ANOTHER MAN'S TREASURE

O H NO! THEY'RE GONE," FIONA SAID. She stood in front of the empty stage. "We missed them."

She had been holding Jaq, and now she put him on the stage and sat down next to him, resting her head in her hands.

"What's wrong?" Jaq asked. He couldn't help looking toward the bushes. His own safety was so close.

"Plenthy was going to save me."

"Save you? From what?"

"From having to live with my evil step-uncle Gunther."

"How?"

"You can't imagine what it's like for me," she said, ignoring his question. "Uncle Gunther is so mean, but he's all my mom and I have." Fiona lifted her head out of her hands and looked at Jaq. "My mom is trying to save money so we can get our own place, and she works super-long hours. But Uncle Gunther makes us pay for everything. He even charges my mom for watching me after school, even though I do all his work for him."

"That sounds terrible. How was Plenthy going to save you?" Jaq asked again, because he was curious how someone his size could do anything on this huge, crazy planet.

"We had a deal," Fiona said, and then her eyes went wide. "Oh no! Uncle Gunther is heading this way, and he looks really mad."

Jaq felt the pull of the wormhole—it was so close. He could make a run for it. But instead he hid behind Fiona, nestled beneath her jacket, and hoped the angry giant wouldn't see them.

"He sees me," Fiona said. "Keep still—you're tickling me." Jaq froze.

"Fiona, you little brat!" the angry giant screamed. "You ran off! That's gonna cost you."

"Please, Uncle Gunther," Fiona said, her voice cracking. "I didn't run off. I couldn't go into the men's room with you, so I went upstairs to see if they had any itch cream in the pharmacy."

He was silent for a second. "Well?"

"They do, but I didn't have any money."

"I have to get back to work. Here, go get me some cream." Jaq felt Fiona's arm reach for something. "But bring back the receipt *and* the change. Every cent."

"Okay."

Fiona stood up, keeping Jaq inside her jacket and safe from view. She held him with a gentle hand, but as she hustled away from Gunther, Jaq began to feel sick again. He wasn't sure if it was motion sickness or because he knew they were heading away from the wormhole, and away from safety.

A part of Jaq wanted to ask her to drop him off in the bushes. The wormhole was so close. But he knew he couldn't leave Bonip. That little wipper had never bitten him, not once, and Jaq knew it wasn't because he tasted funny.

Fiona stopped suddenly, and Jaq peeked out of her jacket.

"Look," Fiona said, pointing to a sign on the wall. "Morgo has another show in an hour."

"We can rescue Plenthy?"

"We can try."

"We have to find Bonip, too. We left him in that restaurant."

"Oh! I'm so sorry," Fiona said. "Do you think he's okay?"

"Are you kidding? He's in a sea of food. That's his paradise. Let's get the itch cream, and then we'll find him and make our plan to rescue Plenthy."

"Okay," Fiona said. "I just hope that pharmacy has itch cream. I kind of made that part up."

As we have seen, the people of Yipsmix value glug above nearly all natural resources.

The people of Epsidor Erandi love the rich colors of the minerals from the Hamaryth Mountains, which they crush into powder and mix into body paint. Some rare colors are extremely expensive. People who can paint themselves ultramarine every day are probably richer than the queen.

The people of Zanflid use the shell of the sea thub as currency. Sometimes the thub is still hiding in the shell, and it has very sharp teeth. Zanflidians are not kidding when they say a deal can come back to bite you.

Jaq was about to learn that on Earth, diamonds are highly prized. Fiona passed a jewelry store on the way to the pharmacy and pointed out the shiny gemstones to Jaq.

"Those are diamonds. Plenthy said he'd get me some."

"Those? Yeah, we have lots of those on Yipsmix," Jaq said. "Kids polish them up and give them to their moms on Gratitude Day."

"Well, here on Earth they're really valuable. If I had a few diamonds, I could sell them, and my mom and I could move away from Step-uncle Gunther. That's why we have to save Plenthy."

"I need Plenthy to get my grandpa out of jail," Jaq said.

"And he needs us, too," Fiona said.

They hurried to buy the itch cream and take it back to Gunther, but he wasn't in the restaurant. Fiona left it for him behind the counter and then took Jaq back upstairs to find Bonip.

It wasn't hard to find the little wipper. Fiona held Jaq in front of her, nestled in her jacket, as she walked by the salad bar. Jaq spotted Bonip lying in a heap next to a container marked GUACAMOLE.

"So . . . full," Bonip moaned.

Jaq grabbed him, and they returned to the booth in the back.

When Fiona placed Jaq on the seat, his gaze drifted up toward the underside of the table. All at once he remembered the other reason he'd come back—glug. There it was, a deformed little blob just within his reach. He pulled a sticky string of it down and showed it to Bonip. "Glug!"

Fiona leaned down. "Plenthy used to have me scrape gum off the bottom of the tables. It was so disgusting." She laughed. "He told me that gum is very valuable on your planet, which is funny."

"Why is it funny?"

"Because it's so cheap here. That chicken I gave you cost four dollars." She noticed Jaq's blank look. "Less than a meal at McDonald's?" she tried.

Jaq's brow furrowed in confusion.

"A few songs on iTunes?"

Jaq shook his head.

"Really cheap!"

Jaq smiled and nodded.

"Why do you guys like gum so much?" Fiona asked.

"Because it's sticky and squishy," Jaq said. "Why do you like diamonds so much?"

"Because they're shiny and pretty."

They both shrugged, as if to say, *To each his own.*

"So Plenthy was collecting gum here and bringing it back to Yipsmix?" Jaq asked. This was Jaq's plan, too.

"At first," Fiona said. "But what he really wanted to do was grow a sapodilla tree on Yipsmix. You can make gum out of the sap of that tree. But I think he was having trouble getting it to work on your planet. The trees would die, and he kept running out of seeds. That's when I met him. He asked me to get some seeds from one of the trees in this restaurant." She pointed to some decorative trees along the wall.

"Glug . . . from trees?" Jaq said. "That's crazy! Glug is a synthetic product."

"Mostly, but we can make gum from trees here, too," Fiona said. "Anyway, I asked the owners—they're really nice—and they gave me the seeds. Plenthy said he'd give me a diamond in exchange for each seed. That was our deal."

"What happened after you gave Plenthy the seeds?" Jaq asked.

"He disappeared! All this time I've been thinking about how stupid I was to believe that someone would trade diamonds for seeds. I mean, really, it sounds so ridiculous.

"But you saw him!" she went on, full of excitement. "If he's here, then maybe he didn't ditch me. He might have my diamonds. We just have to get him away from Morgo the Magnificent."

"How are we going to do that?" Jaq asked.

Fiona's excitement seemed to leak out of her, and she slouched in her seat. "I don't know," she said.

They were quiet for a moment, thinking, and then Bonip bounced up from the vinyl seat to the tabletop. "Plenthy mouthed the word *music* when he saw Jaq waving at him. Right before he warned us about the giant Gunther."

"*Music?*" Fiona said. "That's strange."

"Did you hear that song that was playing during his act?" Jaq asked Bonip.

Bonip nodded. "Catchy tune, easy to dance to—I'd give it an eight. It got weird at the end."

"No, it was . . . different. It gave me chills. The shapes and colors and swirls in it were so . . . precise." Jaq shook his head in awe. "It started with a flowy bit, and then the music rose up, but in a soft and floaty way that made my heart feel light, and then I saw these bursts of red, like giant round berries. It was so surprising. There were more vivid images, but I can't remember them. And then the song ended with darkness."

He shivered and turned to Bonip, who was looking at him like he was crazy. "That's the most ridiculous thing I've ever heard," Bonip said. "It was a song. It had a snazzy beat. That's all."

"I need to hear it again," Jaq said. "And you're right—it really did have a snazzy beat."

Fiona pulled a light blue metallic square out of her pocket. It was no bigger than Jaq's head, with a circle in the middle and a long cord sticking out of one side. The cord split into two, and each side ended with a round plastic bit with a hole at the end.

"I have a ton of songs on here," she said. "It's my old iPod Shuffle. We could listen, if you like. Maybe we'll find the song."

She flipped through a few songs while Jaq held on to one of the earbuds, but nothing sounded like the song Jaq had heard. "This music looks too jumbled."

"What did the other song look like to you?" Fiona asked.

Jaq peeked out of the booth. "Lift me up for a second," he told her. She stood up and held him under her jacket, so he could peek out but still be hidden from view. "See that guy's plate over there?" Jaq said, pointing. The man had his back to them, but the plate on his table was visible. It was filled with different colors and textures and shapes.

"Yeah—that's their Grande Taco Salad Supreme," Fiona said.

"Your music looks like that plate of food. When I listen,

I see a jumbled mess of colors and shapes and tastes. Red blobs, green swirls, tan triangles, and other stuff, all mixed together. The song I heard during the magic act was more like that," he said, pointing to the salad bar, where all the ingredients were laid out in a line. "It made pictures that were ordered and neat, with each one separate from the next."

Fiona sat back down. She was about to ask Jaq a question, when a familiar voice boomed through the restaurant.

"Fiona! What the heck?"

Her step-uncle was storming through the restaurant, right at them.

22

DO YOU HEAR THAT?
IT'S VANILLA

F IONA DROPPED JAQ ONTO THE SEAT, AND
from there he jumped to the floor and hid behind
the table support. His heart beat so fast, it felt like it
was trying to escape his chest and run for safety. He closed
his eyes and listened to the giants.

"I have *had* it with you," Gunther said. "You know I'm suf-
fering, and you're just sitting here! I feel so sick, so nauseous.
And itchy!"

"I got you the cream—"

"You just left it in my restaurant," Gunther said. "How am I supposed to put it on myself? On my back?"

"You . . . you want *me* to put it on your back?" Fiona's voice sounded so faint and weak. It was as if she were being asked to clean an overflowing porta potty, or something equally sad and disgusting.

"Yes. You're supposed to be available when I need you, not roaming around doing whatever you like. I've given you way too much freedom. You're staying in *my* restaurant from now on. I've got to lie down or I'm going to throw up. I can't even think of a good punishment for you—that's how sick I am."

Jaq heard Fiona's voice fade away as she tried to explain herself while being pulled out of the restaurant.

She was gone, and Jaq was stuck. If he tried to leave, one of the giants would surely spot him, and then . . . Jaq shivered, imagining the feeling of being grabbed and squeezed and lifted high in the air again. In other words, complete horror. Even if he could leave unseen, he had no idea how to find the wormhole. Sure, he had a fantastic sense of direction, but that was on Yipsmix. Being on Earth had thrown his senses into a tizzy. Plus, he'd hidden beneath Fiona's coat for most of the trip upstairs. He couldn't retrace steps he hadn't seen.

He slumped to the floor, terrified. In his mind, there was

no chance of survival now that his one giant helper was gone.

Bonip hopped down beside him. "Well, that's a bummer," he said. "Now what?"

"I can't go out there," Jaq said. "Someone will grab me."

"So we stay? I can live with that. Did you see all the food up there?"

"I can't stay. My mom will be so worried. I need to be home by dinner."

"What, then?"

"We wait. When this place is empty, we run for the door. You go first and tell me if it's clear. Nobody notices you, because you're tiny here."

Bonip nodded.

And so they waited. Bonip occasionally hopped over to the salad bar and brought back little bites for Jaq. But Jaq was too nervous to eat, and he sat there tapping his hands on his thighs, dreading the time when he'd have to make a run for it.

After what seemed like ages but was closer to an hour, Fiona returned. Jaq was so grateful, he felt like kissing her shoe.

"My mom got off early and came to pick me up," she said. "She's eating downstairs. But, guys, we missed Morgo's last act."

"Oh, no," Jaq said.

"I know. But someone in the restaurant says he performs all the time. We can try to find him tomorrow."

"Did you hear the song?"

"No, sorry. Uncle Gunther made me watch the restaurant while my mom helped him with the cream, thank goodness. He doesn't trust his workers, so he has me spy on them. Here." She pulled out her music machine. "Take my iPod Shuffle. I'm getting a new one for my birthday, anyway. See if you can find the song. You press the play button in the middle, and the arrow buttons to go forward or back."

"Really? Thanks, Fiona." Jaq lifted the music player with both hands. He was just able to fit it inside his backpack. There was a bit of room left, which reminded him that he'd wanted to fill it with glug. "Can I ask you another favor?"

"Sure," Fiona said.

"Would you mind scraping some gum off the tables for me?" Jaq asked.

"That won't work," Fiona said. "Plenthy tried it. With all sorts of gum, too. Something about going through the wormhole, or just being on your planet, made the Earth gum turn to dust after a couple of days. That's why he wanted to start the tree farm."

"So all that gum in the chicken . . . ?"

"Will soon be dust."

Jaq should have been happy that the Vilcot thieves stole worthless dust, but he wasn't. Bringing back glug was his only hope of saving his family from starvation. But he had no Plenthy and no glug, either. This trip was turning out to be a disaster.

He slumped in the seat. "What do we do now?" he wondered out loud.

"Aww, you look so sad," Fiona said. "Don't worry. We'll see him at the next show. I know we will."

At that moment, Jaq felt an idea sparkle in his brain. "Do all Earthies like diamonds?" he asked.

"Definitely."

"What if I bring back some diamonds? Do you think you could find Morgo and offer a trade?"

"Yes! That's a great idea," Fiona said.

Perfect! It would be so easy to collect a backpack full of diamonds. And then Jaq could free Plenthy, and they could return to Yipsmix together. Plenthy would tell Vilcot he hadn't swindled him, that he'd been trying to find a way to grow glug trees on Yipsmix, as ridiculous as that sounded. It might be enough to make the Vilcots leave them alone and get Grandpa out of jail.

"Come on," Fiona said. "We can check downstairs for his next act, and then I'll take you to the plants."

Jaq was so relieved, he nearly fainted when he stood up.

"Maybe I should get you some food first," Fiona said. "I'll grab some stuff from the salad bar. I know the owners, and they always give me food. Here, jump in my backpack." She held it open, and Jaq crawled inside. "I can show you around a bit while you eat. My mom won't mind." She wore her backpack on her front, so Jaq could peek out from a small gap in the zipper. Bonip perched on his shoulder.

Because it was getting late, the hallways were less crowded now, and Fiona walked at a leisurely pace, taking time to point out to Jaq the things that Plenthy had found interesting. Jaq's mood gradually improved as they toured a toy store, bought chocolate in a candy shop, and sampled some ice cream.

"Try this," she said, holding a tiny (for her) spoon up to Jaq's mouth.

Jaq licked the cold treat. "Wow!" he said. "Do you hear what it's saying?"

"It's ice cream," she said. "It doesn't talk."

Jaq took another lick, and his head nearly burst with joy. "Of course it doesn't talk," he said. "It sings."

By the time they reached the moving staircase, Jaq's belly was full and he'd filled his backpack with treats.

Fiona pointed at a woman standing downstairs by the golden-arches restaurant talking with Gunther. "That's my mom. She's got my stuff and is ready to leave. Do you want me to take you back to the plants?"

Jaq nodded.

They went down the moving staircase, and Fiona edged behind the long row of plants. The sight of Gunther made Jaq's heart thump with panic. He remembered the feeling of being yanked into the air, having his ribs squeezed tight, and staring into that angry face.

"He's dressed differently," Jaq said, noticing that Gunther had changed out of his red shirt and was now wearing a crisp white shirt with a gold badge on the front. He was still scratching like crazy, and he looked extremely irritated.

"He moonlights as a security guard," Fiona said. "Sometimes I have to stay with him until my mom is done working, but I get to skateboard around the mall, which is fun."

"Don't let him see me," Jaq said.

"I won't. I'll go check the performance schedule." Fiona pointed to the stage. She placed Jaq and Bonip in the plants. "Wait here a sec."

Jaq and Bonip hid in the bushes. They were very close to the wormhole, so Jaq felt safe. He watched as Fiona ran over to her mother, grabbing a board with wheels on the bottom. She rode it over to the stage, gliding across the floor with graceful speed. In no time, she was back with Jaq.

"What's that?" he asked, pointing to the board.

"My skateboard," Fiona said. "But listen, they just put up a new sign. That Shrinking Magician trick of Morgo's has gotten him some attention, and he's moving to Reno! He's putting on one final act tomorrow."

"Where's Reno?" Jaq asked.

"It's in Nevada," Fiona said.

That meant nothing to Jaq. Fiona noticed the blank look on his face, so she added, "Really far away!"

"One final act?" Jaq said. "Then we have to move fast. I'll get the diamonds and bring them right back."

"It has to be tomorrow, when Morgo's here. Come back at the same time as these last two days. Any earlier and I'll still be at school."

"Any later and . . ." Jaq didn't have to finish the sentence. Any later and Plenthy would be gone.

"Good luck," Fiona said.

Jaq grabbed Bonip and dove into the wormhole.

23

IT SMELLS ANGRY
IN HERE

THIS TIME, GOING THROUGH THE WORM-
hole was even more painful and terrifying. Jaq felt
his body being pulled apart so violently that when
he landed, he had to make sure all his limbs were still with
him. He noticed that the shimmering oval definitely looked
dimmer.

"That was horrible," he said.

Bonip didn't say anything, and the reason he didn't say
anything was because he had passed out. Jaq put his ear to
the wipper's mouth and pressed lightly on his chest. "Bonip?"

Bonip sucked in air and sat up. "Ack! Never again."

Jaq silently agreed. In making his plan with Fiona, he'd forgotten about how the wormhole seemed to be disappearing, and how going through it was more torturous each time. But he knew he'd have to go through it again. He looked back at the hole, thinking about Fiona. "I have to get the diamonds to Fiona tomorrow. In the meantime, I've got no glug and no way to save my family's farm. Grandpa's still in jail, and poor Plenthy is stuck on that awful planet, a prisoner. And I really, really don't want to go back."

"Maybe you can send your backpack through, filled with the diamonds. Fiona will find it—if it doesn't disintegrate, like I almost did. Then she'll save Plenthy. She can take the diamonds to his next show and buy him off Morgo."

Jaq thought about his options, and the more he thought about it, the more he liked Bonip's plan. That was all he could do, really. Collect the diamonds, send them to Fiona, and hope that she found them. She would be looking for him at the same time the next day; he'd wait until then to send them through, just to make sure nobody else found them first.

They began the hike down the hill. Jaq was completely exhausted. The iPod was heavy on his back, but knowing he had a plan gave him energy for the walk home.

As they walked through the marketplace, Jaq spotted Tormy Vilcot sitting by the fountain, staring at him. Jaq hustled away from Tormy, taking the long way around the fountain. He gripped the straps of his backpack tightly. He did not want to lose his new music player. He really wanted to find that mysterious song, but if he couldn't find it, he hoped to sell the magical music player so he could buy food for his family.

He had just reached the other side of the fountain when he felt someone grab his backpack and yank him to a stop.

"What are you up to, huh?" Tormy asked. "You're always running through the marketplace with that backpack of yours. I know you don't have any money. What are you doing?"

"None of your business," Jaq said, and he immediately regretted it. He should have made up something boring, because now Tormy was even more curious.

"What's in the backpack?"

"Tormy, leave me alone. You've already stolen everything from us. Just leave me alone." Jaq pulled himself free and walked away, but Tormy ran in front of him and put both hands on his shoulders to stop him.

"It's just so easy," Tormy said, smiling. "All I have to do is say that what you have is mine, and everyone believes me.

And I know you won't put up a fight, because you're a coward. So, what do you have of mine in that backpack, hmm? Or should I call over my grandfather's friend?" He nodded toward a policeman standing on the corner.

Jaq couldn't lose his gift from Fiona. He couldn't let Tormy steal yet another thing from him. He clutched his backpack tighter, but this only made Tormy want it more. Tormy grabbed the backpack, trying to wrestle it off Jaq's shoulders. As he did, the flap flipped open, and out popped Bonip, squeaking.

"It's a wipper!" Tormy shouted. Immediately, everyone in the area raced away from the pair. One man scowled at Tormy, but Tormy just shouted at his back—"Wipper! Wipper! Wipper! I don't care about Contagion! I have a wipper-slinger!"

Jaq closed his backpack and put it back on.

"That's really sad," Tormy said, laughing. "Your only friend is a wipper."

Like everyone else, Jaq hurried away from Tormy. This time, only Tormy's laughter chased after him.

Jaq slowed once he reached the road that led to his home. Tormy rode past him on his hoverbike, still laughing and swirling up dust.

"Did I do good?" Bonip asked, climbing up Jaq's leg.

"Huh?" Jaq plucked Bonip off his leg and put him on his shoulder.

"I jumped out so he wouldn't find the music thing," Bonip said. "I thought the squeak was a nice touch. You know—really distracting."

Jaq smiled. "Thanks, Bonip."

He walked on, wishing he had a hoverbike. Tormy would probably finish his dinner before Jaq even reached home. Bonip yawned and ducked into the backpack. Soon, soft snoring sounds surrounded Jaq's head like pastel bubbles.

As he passed the Vilcots' farm, Jaq knew he shouldn't look over, but he did. He saw them in their big front yard—Tormy, his mom and dad, his grandfather, and a crowd of farm workers. They were watching the plastic chicken walk and lay its glug eggs. They all laughed and cheered every time it did. Jaq saw Klingdux whiz around one of those glugballs and sling it across the yard. The Vilcots screamed at poor Klingdux, and Tormy slapped his pet, pushing him to go retrieve the glug.

Jaq wanted to throw rocks at the whole awful family.

Klingdux ran to fetch the ball of glug. He came right up to the fence where Jaq stood.

"Hey there, buddy," Jaq said.

Klingdux stopped and stared at Jaq for a second, but then Tormy screamed at him to come back. Klingdux let out a yip as he turned to hustle the glugball back to his new master.

"That's gotta hurt," Bonip said. He was peeking out of the backpack.

Jaq couldn't answer. He had a huge lump in his throat. He looked down and blinked rapidly. Then he kicked the ground and continued for home.

"Hey, he's just a dumb animal," Bonip said. "That bratty kid probably feeds him twelve times a day. Don't take it personally."

"Why shouldn't I?" Jaq said. "I raised him! I gave him my bed, my blanket, and most of my own food. And now he acts like he doesn't even know me. Just like you did. I'm sorry, but I do take it personally. What's wrong with me?"

"There's nothing wrong with you," Bonip said. He looked like he wanted to say more, but Jaq just shook his head.

"You wippers are right," Jaq said. "I'm a funny-looking loser. Davardi's right—I'm just a stupid kid. And Tormy's right—I'm a coward and I have no friends."

Bonip hopped up onto Jaq's shoulder and punched him on the cheek. "You're pretty good at turning off the noise on Earth," he said. "You need to do it here, too. Why are you listening to wippers, swindlers, and brats? Why are you letting them decide who you are? *You* need to decide who you are, or who you want to be. Nobody can decide who you are but you."

"I can't pretend to be brave when I'm not," Jaq said.

"You *are* brave! You went back to Earth even though you knew it was filled with giants."

"I also let Tormy steal my chicken. I didn't fight at all, and they took Grandpa away!"

"How could you fight them? You were outnumbered eight-to-one. By grown-ups!"

Near the gate, Jaq picked Bonip off his shoulder and placed him on the ground. "You probably don't want to be seen with me."

Bonip looked up at him. "Jaq—"

Jaq waved his hand and went inside.

Back at the Vilcot farm, Klingdux was still struggling to get out of Tormy's grasp so he could chase after Jaq.

Inside, Jaq's mother greeted him with a hug.

"No glug?" she asked Jaq.

Jaq shook his head. "It turns out it's fool's glug. It will turn to dust in a couple of days."

She slumped back into her chair. "I just don't know what else to do. I don't know how we can save the farm."

"How's Grandpa?"

"Still in jail. Vilcot told me he'd drop the charges against Grandpa if I sold the farm to him."

"What did you say?"

"It was funny, actually. I wish you could have been there. I told him that Grandpa is very happy in jail. They feed him there, and because of his age, he doesn't have to do any work. I thanked Vilcot for his offer but declined." She even laughed. "I thought he was going to spasm with rage. I have a feeling he's dropping the charges right about now."

Jaq smiled. He looked out the window at the fence that separated their land from the Vilcots' farm, with its tall, healthy trees just dripping with fruit. But in front of the fence, on the Rollop side, there was nothing but dusty, barren land.

"It doesn't matter," Jaq said, giving the wall a frustrated kick. "We're going to have to sell this place, aren't we?"

"Yes."

"And Vilcot will buy it, won't he?"

"Yes."

"Where will we live?"

Mom had no answer for that.

Jaq gave her the chocolates he'd brought back from Earth, and for a brief moment they were happy.

"I wish I hadn't made you sell Klingdux, Jaq," his mother said, drifting off to sleep. "Oh, Jaq, I dream of being able to buy you all the things you want. Wait, no. Then you'd be a spoiled brat like that Tormy Vilcot. Let's say I dream of being able to buy you one or two of the things you want. Because I love you and you're a good kid."

She was asleep before he could answer.

PLAY THAT PURPLE
SONG AGAIN

THE NEXT MORNING, JAQ'S MOTHER GOT up early to go to work. Jaq thought she looked so tired; the burden of saving their family had worn her down. After she left, Jaq decided to skip school. He was too distracted to pay attention to anything anyway.

He stood on the back porch, gazing at the fields. His family was going to lose their farm. It might be small and difficult, but it was theirs. The one-room shack was theirs. He knew the feel of the soil, the earthy-woody smell of his ripweed field, and all the familiar sights—the amber fields, the trees growing by the dry riverbed, with their brown trunks and parchment-colored leaves, the caramel and cream-colored hills beyond the river.

He didn't want to lose it all, but there was no fighting it now. Even if he rescued Plenthy, even if Plenthy told mean, old Vilcot that Grandpa hadn't stolen his money, it wouldn't give them money to keep their farm.

Still, he *had* to help rescue Plenthy. Nobody deserved to be trapped on Earth.

Jaq sat on the back porch and listened to the songs on the iPod, but none of them painted a clear picture like that other song had. The songs were all Grande Taco Salad Supreme. Not a single Salad Bar in the mix. There were blasts and swirls and smells, but they gave him a random mishmash of senses. An explosion of red pops coupled with . . . the smell of cut grass? The music made no sense.

And then, as he tended his side garden, the hose dripped some water onto the iPod and it stopped working altogether. No matter how hard he pushed on the buttons, nothing happened. What kind of people made something that broke after a little water touched it? That was ridiculous! And now Fiona's gift was worthless to him—not only was it broken, but he hadn't been able to find the song he wanted.

Frustrated, Jaq picked up a rock and threw it into the field.

"Hey, fat-foot." A sharp voice emerged from the stalks. "Where are the worms, huh? We're hungry over here."

"The Vilcots moved the river," Jaq answered. "My worming spot has dried up."

"So walk a little farther and find a new one," another wipper said. "How lazy can one guy be? Jeez."

Jaq got up to go back inside. He didn't have to take this abuse anymore.

"You'd be slow and lazy, too," another one said, "if you had to drag around that enormous head."

Laughter filled the air, until . . .

"Hey, cut it out."

Jaq turned around. Bonip had crept out of the stalks and stood in front of the insulting wipper.

"What did you say, Bonip?"

"You heard me, Drixo. I said: Cut . . . it . . . out. Why are you picking on him? Can't you see he's miserable? This guy has been getting us worms for months, and all you do is insult him. That's mean."

Jaq couldn't believe it. Nobody had ever stuck up for him before. Not here, not at school, not anywhere. He wanted to reach down and hug the little wipper.

"Mean?" Drixo said. "Me? I'm the nicest guy here. Just

yesterday I helped Egbot clean out his nest. He didn't even ask me to."

"That's not how it works," Bonip said. "You can't be mean all day, and then just because you do one nice thing that makes you a nice guy. A nice guy wouldn't say a cruel thing, ever. Not one mean thing, not ever. You, Drixo, are not nice. I'm not nice, either, because I turned my back on that giant fat-foot when he needed a friend. But I'm going to stand up for him now. And if that makes you guys hate me, then hate me."

"What's going on?" Another wipper peeked out of the stalks. Jaq recognized him as the ringleader of the bunch.

"Nothing, Hedgemud," Drixo said.

Bonip didn't say anything. None of the other wippers said anything, either.

"Well, I'm feeling like we gotta go next door," the wipper leader said. "I just scouted over there. Nice, rich soil. We may have to dig a bit harder, but I bet there are worms over there. Plus, I feel this crazy tug pulling me in that direction."

Contagion by Mention, Jaq thought.

"Okay, let's go," Drixo said. The wippers quickly scurried off toward the Vilcots' farm.

Bonip looked up at Jaq. Jaq smiled and nodded toward the fence. "I don't have any food for you here," he said.

"You want me to help you get back to the waterfall later?" Bonip asked.

"That's okay," Jaq said. "I can make it. Thanks, though."

Bonip nodded and crouched down, compressing his back legs. And then he took off like something shot from a catapult. Those wippers could almost fly, they jumped so far.

After the wippers left, Jaq got to work collecting foot scrapers. As he hunted for the diamonds, he thought about Bonip's plan. He knew it was logical, but a little part of him couldn't help but think that he was a coward for staying on Yipsmix. Then he remembered how frightening it was to go through that wormhole. And what, exactly, could he do if he went through with the diamonds? Nothing.

He piled a small mound of diamonds on the porch. The stupid rocks were so worthless, Jaq had no idea how many Fiona would need. He'd found all the ones that were close to the house.

He had just returned from the old riverbed with two huge rocks when his mom arrived home early from work. Jaq followed her inside, where she collapsed into her chair.

"They fired me," she said. "I made too many mistakes because I've been so tired."

"Oh no," Jaq said.

She got right back up again. "But I'm not giving up, Jaq. I'm going to the bank to see if I can get a new loan and get Vilcot off our back. Will you be okay here alone?"

Jaq nodded.

"I'm not giving up," she said again.

But before she could reach the door, the ground started to shake. Thumps rocked the house, and the air shimmered with flashes of light. Jaq and his mom stepped outside and saw the Vilcots riding their Arbians up to the front door. Jaq looked up at them, perched so high on their mounts.

"I'm here to inform you that you must vacate the premises by tomorrow," Ripley Vilcot said. "I've purchased your loan from the bank, and I'm foreclosing. Don't know why I didn't think of this sooner. You have one day to pay what's owed or vacate. Please be gone by tomorrow night."

Jaq and his mom were too stunned to say anything.

"By nightfall," Vilcot repeated. He took something out of his pocket. It was another key, just like the one Jaq had traded for Klingdux. "And you can give this to Greggin," he said, throwing the key at Jaq's feet. "Tell him that his friend is not getting the last laugh with his little mocking gifts. *I* get the last laugh."

He rode off laughing.

25

COURAGE SPARKLES LIKE A STAR—AND LIKE A STAR, IT SEEMS OUT OF REACH

JAQ PICKED UP THE KEY. HIS MOM PUT A HAND on his shoulder. "I have to go," she said. "There must be someone in town who hates the Vilcots as much as I do and will lend us the money."

She left Jaq alone.

Jaq opened the key, like Grandpa had shown him. Inside was another note:

Dear Yorlim Plenthy's friend,
My name is Dharvil, and I work for Plenthy at one of his glug

*farms. I need to find him, quickly. I remembered how he'd asked
me to take that other key to your farm in case of emergency. I
hope that key worked, and I hope you get this one, too. If you are
anything like my boss, you must also love puzzles, like this key.
That Plenthy and his puzzles!*

*You see, Plenthy has been missing for a while now, and I
need some direction. The trees are glugging like mad, and the
warehouse is full. Should I sell the glug or rent out more space?
Like I said, I need an answer quickly, as we are drowning in glug.
What a problem to have, ha!*

> *Yours,*
>
> *Dharvil Meyr, First Rancher for Farm Three*

Jaq reread the note. He turned it over to see if there was
any indication of where it had come from or who this Dharvil
was. Nothing.

This was crazy. The glug-tree idea had worked? Jaq stared
blinking at the fields as the news seeped into his thoughts
and exploded into one gigantic realization: Plenthy was rich!
He could save them—if Jaq saved him.

Jaq hurried to collect a few more foot scrapers. He couldn't
stop thinking about the note.

That Plenthy and his puzzles, the note said.

Plenthy had mouthed the word *music* when he saw Jaq hiding in the bushes. What if that strange song with the emotions and pictures was from Plenthy? What if Plenthy was trying to send a message with the song, like a puzzle?

As he searched for the rocks, Jaq tried for the hundredth time to remember the mysterious song. He saw the pictures the song painted, he tasted the notes, he felt the song on his skin. The images were so vivid, he could almost draw them.

Jaq picked up a stick and made swirls in the dust. He doodled while the song played in his head. The splashy-water part, the swirling-up part, the red blobs. There were other parts he couldn't remember, and then the dark part.

He looked at his swirls and pictures. How had he not realized it before? It was so obvious.

The song was a map.

It was a map that only another Yipsmixer could decipher.

"That Plenthy and his puzzles!" Jaq repeated.

He hopped up and down in excitement. The splashy part—that had to be the fountain. The swirling-up part was the moving staircase. But what about the rest? All he could remember was the darkness and the terror at the end.

"BONIP!" he yelled. "The song's a map! It's a map! Bonip! We can find him!"

But Bonip was gone. And Jaq didn't have much time.

He bundled up the diamonds in a towel and stuffed it into his backpack. He was ready to go.

He knew, deep down, that if he went ahead with his plan to send the backpack through while staying safely behind, that someone else might find it, or that Fiona might find it but not in time. On the other hand, he knew that if he told himself he was going through the wormhole, panic and fear would grip him so tightly that he wouldn't be able to leave the house.

Jaq needed to find some courage to go through the wormhole and rescue Plenthy himself. The best way to capture a shy beast like courage is to sneak up on it and grab it before it knows what's coming, so Jaq continued to tell himself that he was taking the safe route, because that would get him to the wormhole. He tried not to think about going through the wormhole himself, because that would startle his courage, and it would flee.

You decide who you want to be.

That was what Bonip had said. Jaq wanted to be courageous. He wanted to save Plenthy.

As he neared his front gate, he heard a scream from the other side of the fence.

"Wipper-slinger!"

Jaq smiled. Klingdux must be getting to work. He heard more screaming, and then a small white ball of fluff flew over the fence. It was headed right for his best brickleberry bush. Without thinking, Jaq dropped his backpack and ran. He ran and dove and caught the rodent just before it crashed into his bush. He cradled the wipper as he rolled to the ground, so it wouldn't be hurt. Then he stood up and placed it gently on the ground.

"Hey, thanks," the wipper said.

But Jaq wasn't looking at him. He was watching the sky as another wipper came over the fence. He caught that one, too, and dropped it to the ground just as another came flying at him. Wippers continued to rain down. Jaq ran to the left, and he ran to the right. He raced and dove and smiled, because it was really fun. He didn't miss a single wipper.

"He can run forever," one of the wippers said.

"And that hand-eye coordination is like nothing I've ever seen."

"He's got gentle hands, too. Didn't squish me at all."

There was a pause in the slinging, and Jaq took a moment to glance down. All the wippers were looking up at him. Their mouths were open in awe.

"Bonip was right," the one named Drixo said. "This kid's okay." He clapped his hands together, slowly at first. Then the rest joined in.

Jaq couldn't believe it. The wippers were applauding him. He looked at each one but didn't see Bonip among them.

"Where's Bonip?" he asked.

"He's coming. The wipper-slinger always saves his best sling for last, and Bonip wanted to make sure he got your attention."

And then they heard it: Bonip screaming, "Jaaaaaaaaq!"

He flew over the fence, over the brickleberry bushes, all the way to the side of Jaq's house, where he slammed into the wall and fell to the porch. Jaq ran over.

"Bonip, are you okay?"

"I . . . heard . . . what . . . you said," he whispered. "The song's a map."

"It is!"

"I want to go with you," Bonip said.

"Of course. Let's go!"

"Can I have a second? I just flew across your yard and into this wall here."

"I'll carry you," Jaq said to the prone wipper. "Let's go!"

∗

Jaq started at a run—he was sure he didn't have much time. The visit from the Vilcots had cut into his schedule. He ran out the gate and down the road, but carrying a heavy backpack full of diamonds quickly wore him out and he had to walk to catch his breath. That was when Tormy Vilcot tackled him.

"Where you going, twiggy?" Tormy said while sitting on Jaq's back. "Shouldn't you be packing up?"

"Tormy, get off," Jaq said.

"I'm not going to," Tormy said. "My grandfather told me not to let you go anywhere. He's afraid you'll find another one of those glug birds. With all that glug, you could probably save your farm."

"The bird's worthless," Jaq said. "The glug turns to dust."

"Yeah, sure it does," Tormy said. "Looks like you lost your buddy." Bonip had run off as soon as Jaq had been flattened. "I have a little worm you can have for a friend. That would suit you."

Jaq lay there, unable to move. Why did the Vilcots have to ruin everything?

"Since we'll be sitting here for a while, let me tell you about my plans for your little hut," Tormy went on. "It's going to be my second playroom, and I'm going to fill it with toys—"

Jaq tried not to listen. Maybe Tormy would shift his weight and Jaq could wiggle free. He knew he could outrun Tormy if he could escape. Maybe not with a backpack filled with rocks, but he could collect more once he'd gotten away.

But he couldn't move, and Tormy kept going on and on. Jaq felt a futile anger rise up in him as he realized that he wasn't going to make it to the wormhole in time.

"—and after the pool is finished, I'm going to invite the whole class over for a party. It's going to be great, the—"

Jaq opened his eyes to see why Tormy had stopped talking.

"What are they doing?" Tormy said. "They're coming this way."

Jaq followed his gaze. White blobs were springing toward them. Beautiful, angry white rodents with sharp teeth.

"Gah!" Tormy jumped off Jaq and raced away before the gang of wippers arrived. They surrounded Jaq as he sat up.

"That was easy," Bonip said. "A skeleton has more guts than that guy."

The other wippers all cheered Bonip's insult. It was an oldie but a goodie.

"Thanks, guys," Jaq said. He grabbed his backpack. "Bonip, we've gotta run."

"We're all going," the leader, Hedgemud, said. "Every

time Bonip comes back from one of your trips, he looks like he's eaten a feast. We want in."

"Yeah, stop skipping out on us, already," one of the wippers said.

"Where are you going?" another asked. "Is it far?"

"We're going through a wormhole—"

Before Jaq could explain further, the wippers started jumping with excitement.

"I knew it would be something fantastic!"

"A hole full of worms!"

Jaq shushed them. "It's not full of worms. It's like a tunnel to another planet. We're going to try to rescue someone. I'm not sure there will be food."

"We're going," Drixo said. All the wippers stood with their paws on their hips. They looked fiercely determined.

"Guys," Jaq said, "it's painful to go through. And really dangerous."

"If Bonip trusts you, we trust you," Hedgemud said. "Lead the way, Bigfoot."

26

A DRIVING SENSE
OF URGENCY

J
AQ RACED UP THE TRAIL, SILENTLY PRAYING to Smolders that they weren't too late. That Fiona was still at the mall. That Plenthy wasn't on his way to Reno, wherever that was. His legs ached, but he kept pushing on, as fast as he could move.

In the cave behind the waterfall, he finally stopped to catch his breath. He removed his earmuffs and earplugs. Then he took off his backpack and looked at it. It would be so easy just to throw it into the wormhole and be done with it. It would be so easy to hope that things would work out. It would be so easy to convince himself that he'd done everything a small person could do.

But he knew better. He knew that hoping and good intentions weren't the same thing as doing and making sure.

He thought about Fiona and how she wanted to trade the diamonds to free a friend, even though she could use them to save herself and her mother from Gunther. She was going to sacrifice her own happiness to save Plenthy.

He thought about Bonip, and how the little wipper had stuck up for him against the whole big gang of wippers.

And he thought of his mother, who didn't give up, even when everything seemed lost.

He realized then where courage really came from. It didn't come from having superpowers or an indestructible suit or a powerful weapon—those were cheats. Courage came from caring about something, or someone, more than you cared about yourself.

And the things Jaq cared about most were saving his family, saving Plenthy, saving Fiona, and saving his farm. They were all counting on him, and he couldn't let them down.

He took a deep breath and put his backpack back on.

"So we're doing it?" Bonip said. "We're going through?"

"I have to," Jaq said, standing in front of a much dimmer

wormhole. "Bonip, you guys can stay here. You don't have to come."

"If you're going, we're all going," Bonip said. He climbed up Jaq's leg and positioned himself on his shoulder, clinging to his neck. The other wippers held on as well.

Jaq smiled and nodded. "All right—here goes."

Going through the wormhole was just as terrible as Jaq knew it would be. The pain in his head and the ripping-apart sensation were even worse this time. He landed on the soft Earth soil, unable to breathe. It felt like he'd gotten the wind knocked out of him, been trampled by a herd of gows, and then had every limb yanked to its breaking point. He hurt all over, and not just because he was covered in moaning wippers.

"Ouch," Bonip said. "I can't move."

"Me, neither," Jaq said. He closed his eyes. The burbling fountain filled his head with soft swirls of color. "Ugh," he said at last. "How are we ever going to do that again?"

"One more time," Bonip said. "It's got to work one more time. I know it will."

Jaq wasn't so sure. The wormhole was barely a flicker now.

It took a while, but finally the pain in Jaq's head began to ease. He threw off his heavy backpack and the last of the wippers who were clinging to him. He peeked out of the bushes and saw a darker and quieter mall. Jaq didn't see a single giant. His heart sank. They were too late. Fiona was gone.

"This is it?" Hedgemud said. Twelve furry heads poked out next to him.

Jaq pulled the bundle of diamonds out of his backpack and buried it in the dirt, placing a stick straight up near the pile. He put his lighter backpack back on. He'd packed a flashlight and some rope, the only rescue supplies he could find.

Just as he was about to jump out of the bushes, a *clack–clack–clack* sound headed their way. He ducked back just as a giant came into view.

"Gunther," Bonip whispered. He turned to the other wippers. "Big and mean, and he tastes like that smelly kid next door with the sweaty socks."

"Ew."

"Shh," Jaq said. Time seemed to slow down as he watched the grabby giant walk by their hiding spot. Was he hesitating? Was he looking their way? Why couldn't he walk faster? The echoes of Gunther's steps vibrated through Jaq's body— *thump . . . thump . . . thump*—while Jaq's heart was speeding away—*thumpthumpthumpthump*. His feet wanted to speed away, too.

Slowly, very slowly, Gunther passed the bushes and continued down the first-floor corridor. Jaq watched the giant walk beyond the moving staircase. Finally he was able to let out the breath he'd been holding, and when he did, he noticed something across the way.

"Look," Jaq said, pointing to the restaurant with the two golden arches. "There's a light on over there. I'm hearing and seeing something coming from inside."

"Let's go," Bonip said. "Follow my lead, guys. If you see a crunchy stick on the floor, it's delicious. The green leafy stuff, not so much."

The wippers jumped down and bounced across the hallway.

Jaq ran after them, keeping his eyes on Gunther's back as the giant walked away. They quickly made it to the restaurant, and Jaq saw what was making the noise.

Fiona sat in a booth, her head in her hands. She was crying. Faint maroon swirls danced around her head and drifted up in the air as her body shook with sobs.

"Fiona?" Jaq said.

Her head whipped up.

"Jaq!" she said, wiping her eyes with the back of her hand. "You came back!" She kneeled down on the floor and looked him in the eye. "Thank goodness. And, look, more white fluffy guys!"

Bonip didn't look happy. "Hey, the floor is clean," he said angrily. "Where's the food?"

Fiona reached up to the table and grabbed a red carton. When she shook it, a faint clatter echoed from inside. "I have some fries left," she said.

The wippers all jumped toward her, so she placed the carton on the tabletop, and soon they were swarming over it.

"I'm so sorry I'm late," Jaq said to Fiona. "I meant to come back at the right time, but I got tackled by a horrible boy next door, and he wouldn't let me go. And now Plenthy is gone."

"Maybe not," she said. "Listen, I think I figured it out."

"The song's a map," they both said at the same time.

They both laughed. Fiona picked Jaq up and put him on the table, which was covered with papers and books and wippers.

"I figured it out after you left. I kept wondering why he'd say *music* when he saw you. And then, when you described the images . . . it just made sense. So I recorded it today with my mom's iPhone," she said. "I don't see the same things you do, but I thought if you came back, we could figure it out together."

"What about Gunther?"

"He's doing his rounds. I'm supposed to be writing up his hourly log." She lifted the paper. "He comes in now and then to tell me that he hasn't seen anything. This will go on for a couple more hours, and then my mom will pick me up after her late shift is over."

"So we're safe here?"

"Yes. If he comes by, just duck behind my backpack until he leaves. Now let's listen to the song."

She pulled a device out of her backpack. It was much bigger than the one she'd given Jaq. When she pressed the front, Jaq heard the song again.

"Okay, tell me what you see," Fiona said, pencil ready.

"There's the splashy, watery part that must be that fountain," Jaq said. "And here comes the rising-up part."

"The escalator," Fiona said.

"And then big popping red circles."

"Got it," she said. "Next?"

"It's peaceful. All earth tones. I feel like I'm surrounded by soft clouds that are gently brushing against my skin. And now comes the spicy part. The sounds are prickling my mouth."

"Like in the Mexican restaurant," Bonip said.

"Yes," Fiona said. "Plenthy *would* use that as a marker. Okay, good. What's next?"

"This part is bubbly. There's a freshness about it."

"The bath store?" Fiona said. "It's just around the corner from the Mexican restaurant."

Jaq relayed each sensation, which Fiona wrote down, and then she added her guess as to which store went with each picture.

"And now this part makes me feel like it's dark and quiet," Jaq said.

"Dark and quiet?"

"Yes, there's a tunnel of darkness, an emptiness."

"Hmm. There's a corridor upstairs where three stores just closed. It's practically deserted. There's only one left at the end, a pet store, it's—"

"Turn it off!" Jaq interrupted.

"But the song's not over."

"I can't take that last part! It's terrifying."

Fiona switched off the song and looked at her paper. "The pet store? That *would* be terrifying to a little guy like Plenthy. What if he's been kept in the pet store this whole time? Maybe he's not gone yet?"

"Can we check?" Jaq asked.

She stood up and held out a hand for him and the wippers.

"Let's go."

27

MUSIC CAN GIVE YOU CHILLS, MAKE YOU CRY, OR KNOCK YOU OUT IN TERROR

FIONA HELD JAQ WHILE THE WIPPERS CLUNG to her sleeve. She grabbed her skateboard and headed for the escalator, keeping an eye out for Gunther.

"I don't see him, but this is a huge mall," she said.

Once they reached the second floor, Fiona put down her board, and they were off. She said the names of the stores they'd marked on the map as she zoomed past them.

"Round red popping—balloons!—the party store!"

"The spa store!"

"The Mexican restaurant!"

They turned a corner.

"Bed, Soaps, and Stuff!"

"Uh-oh," she said more quietly. "Uncle Gunther."

Jaq looked up and saw the angry giant striding toward them. Fiona stuffed Jaq into her jacket pocket.

"Um . . . hi, Uncle Gunther!" Fiona said, waving.

He scowled at her, and then they were past.

"The dark corridor is ahead," she said.

Jaq peeked out of the pocket. "Do you see that?"

"I don't know," Bonip said from Jaq's shoulder. "Is there something to see? Or are you hearing something? Or tasting something? Or touching something?"

"Noise," Jaq replied. "That corridor across the way. There are stripes and blasts of very faint colors. Let's go."

Fiona hurried toward the sound at the end of the hallway while Jaq silently prayed that it was the right spot.

The sounds grew louder and brighter as they reached the end of the corridor. Fiona put a foot down, and they stopped in front of a glass-fronted store filled with living creatures in wire pens. The colors in Jaq's vision were coming from the chirps, barks, mews, and other noises from the animals in the cages.

"This *has* to be it," he said. "Do you hear it? It's still noisy in there, even though everywhere else is quiet."

"How do we get in?" Bonip asked.

Fiona tried the door, but it was locked.

"There," Jaq said, pointing. He had seen that the sounds were sneaking out a hole in the door. It was a narrow, rectangular slot. Jaq could reach the bottom of the opening if he raised his hands. The slot was covered with a metal door that swung open when Jaq pushed it.

"Let me boost you guys in so you can look around," Fiona said. "I'll wait out here and stand guard."

"Okay," Jaq said. "Do you want to go first?" he asked Bonip.

"Yeah. We'll tell you if the coast is clear."

Fiona held out her hand for the wippers, then lifted them through the opening. Once Bonip gave the okay, Jaq crawled through, landing on a pile of papers that had been dropped through the slot.

The store was filled with a racket that made Jaq cover his ears. Squawks and chirps and barks punctuated a background of burbling water tanks. Bonip waited by the slot, but the rest of the wippers had spread out in search of more food. Jaq could see little balls of white bounce in the air as they hopped through the store.

Faint light spilled from the tanks, but the rest of the room was dark, especially near the floor. Jaq pulled out his flashlight and swung it around, illuminating cages and tanks that were stacked on top of each other. They stretched from the floor upward, almost as high as he could see. He gasped. They were filled with terrifying creatures.

"No wonder the end of the song was so full of dread," Jaq said. "It's like a store of monsters in cages."

"It's definitely monsterful," Bonip agreed. "Which one do you think Plenthy is in?"

They scanned the tanks near the bottom and saw mostly water-dwelling creatures. "Not there," Jaq said. "He'd drown."

Moving on, they came to cages with furry creatures huddled in big piles, mostly sleeping.

"They're huge!" Jaq said. He backed away from the pens, hurrying to the middle of the aisle.

"What if he's in one of the top cages?" Bonip asked.

"I don't think he'd be there, where anyone could see him," Jaq said. "Maybe there's a back room."

They continued down the aisle and reached the end. On the opposite end of the back wall was a door, so they ran over to it. Jaq held his hands to his ears. "Do you hear that?"

Bonip tilted his head toward the door. "Music?"

"I think so," Jaq said. He let the music into his head, and then he collapsed.

✳

Jaq came back to consciousness with Bonip jumping on his chest yelling, "Wake up! Wake up! Wake up!"

Jaq shoved him off and stood.

"What happened?" Bonip asked.

"That music," Jaq said. "It was filled with sadness, and pain, and terror. It was overwhelming."

"That's probably your guy," Bonip said. "But how do we get in there?"

Jaq approached the door and saw hinges along the side. It was a swinging door. He got down on the floor to look underneath. He could hear voices now.

"—or I'll take it away," said a deep voice.

"Then I'll starve myself, and you'll have no act," another voice said.

"Just play something happier!" the giant voice said. "Or mysterious, like that piece you recorded for the act. I like that one. Anything but that latest piece of garbage. I swear, I'll take that keyboard and mouse out of your cage and you'll have nothing to do but sit. No more GarageBand for you."

"Then I'll starve myself—"

"Stop saying that! And just so you know, there's another one of you running about. A younger one. Gunther told me. When I get my hands on him, I won't need you anymore, you old geezer. I'll feed you to your new neighbor, Squeezer. I'm putting his cage on the desk so you can see what I'll do to you if you don't do exactly what I say."

"Mortimer, you are—"

"MORGO!" Jaq heard something slam. "Don't ever call me Mortimer. I am Morgo the Magnificent."

"You are Mortimer the cruel pet shop manager, nothing more."

"Say hello to Squeezer. Here she comes."

"Hello, Squeezer," the softer voice said. "Tell me, do you despise Mortimer as much as I do?"

"I'm going to get some food," the giant voice said. "If you were nicer, I'd bring you something. But you're not, so all you get is food pellets. Or some of these freeze-dried worms I feed the fish. That'll teach you to cooperate."

"Thank you. That will make it much easier for me to starve myself—"

"Arrgh! Shut up, you stupid old man. We could be rich and famous, if you'd only just work with me."

"Your lust for fame has clouded your sense. It has made you evil. To keep another person prisoner just so you can hear applause is evil. And this act will not work forever, you—"

"I said, shut up! I'm not listening to you anymore. And you're not a person. You're nothing but a pet who can talk."

Jaq heard approaching footsteps, so he ducked behind a shelf just as the door swung open. The giant Mortimer stomped past him and out of the pet shop. Jaq saw that the door was still swinging, so he darted into the back room.

The heartbreaking song started playing again, and Jaq felt himself swooning with sadness. His eyes filled with tears. He was barely able to get his bearings and look around.

The back room was an office. Shelves filled with boxes of all sizes covered the wall that faced the door. Along the wall to Jaq's right was a long desk, and on the desk was a cage, and inside the cage was a very sad Yipsmixer. It was Plenthy. From across the room Jaq could just see him over the edge of the desk. He was staring at a large bright screen positioned just outside his cage. He frowned and then pushed a flattish plastic box around a pad on the floor of his cage. He pushed down on a button on the top of the box, and Jaq heard a click. Music came out of the screen until Plenthy clicked again. The music stopped.

Somehow, Plenthy was making music come out of the screen by rolling a plastic box around on a pad inside his cage. It was like magic.

"Plenthy?" Jaq said.

Plenthy moved to the edge of his cage. "What? Who's that? Who's there?"

"I'm Jaq Rollop, from Yipsmix. I'm here to rescue you. How do I get you out of there?"

"Never mind me!" Plenthy said. "Get out of here! Now!"

"But I've come to save you. I found your note."

"Run, you fool!"

"I'll free you, and we'll both run."

"There's no time! Run! Mortimer's snake is heading right for you!"

28

THIS IS NOT A GOOD TIME TO SENSE THAT YOUR BLADDER IS FULL

J AQ LOOKED WHERE PLENTHY WAS POINTING. Sure enough, at the far end of the desk the giant fang-toothed worm of his nightmares was slowly sliding past the loosely secured lid of its cage and down toward the floor. Every bit of Jaq froze in fear. He couldn't move, he couldn't breathe, he couldn't even form a thought. Terror engulfed him. He watched the hideous monster as its head landed gently on the floor, the rest of its enormous body following with a sickening thump of doom. The beast seemed stuck for a moment, waiting for its body to straighten itself out.

"MOVE!" Bonip yelled right into Jaq's ear.

Jaq's vision filled with a blast of yellow and red sparklers, and that was enough to melt whatever had frozen him. He ran for the door and tried to push it open.

"I can't budge it!" he said. "What do I do?"

"The storage shelf!" Plenthy yelled.

With Bonip clinging to his shoulder, Jaq ran for the shelving unit that faced the door. As the snake slithered toward him, Jaq climbed onto the top of a box on the first shelf. From there he jumped to the second shelf. The boxes were smaller here; some of them had been opened. He grabbed the edge of one . . . and the whole thing tipped over, dumping chew toys and rubber balls to the floor. The next box was almost empty, so Jaq threw it to the floor. Anything to slow that monster down.

The snake wound its way around the obstacles, taking its time because it knew its prey was trapped.

The next box was heavy, but Jaq squeezed behind it and pushed it off the shelf. He looked down just as it hit the floor and broke open, spilling round containers decorated with pictures of fish. He knew he needed to get higher. He tipped another box over to make a step and then climbed on top of it so he could reach the next shelf.

Jaq glanced down and saw the enormous snake's head stretching to the second shelf. It was climbing up with ease.

The third shelf held strange contraptions made of wood and covered with carpet. Perfect! Jaq thought. He climbed up one easily and made it to the fourth shelf, which held a row of books. Now he was a bit higher than the top of the desk.

The snake followed, slithering over boxes much more easily than Jaq had. It was now on the shelf just below him, its head swinging back and forth, searching for its prey.

"Hurry!" Plenthy called, his face as pale as the fingers that gripped the bars of the cage. "Hurry!"

Jaq took off his backpack and removed the rope. "Bonip, I'm going to tie this rope around you and toss you onto the desk. You give that end to Plenthy, and have him tie it to something strong. Then I can swing over."

"Toss me? That's an insult," Bonip said. "I jump farther than that in my sleep." He grabbed the rope with his teeth, crouched down on his back legs, and sprang forward like something shot from a cannon. He landed with a thump and a roll, popping up right next to the wire cage that held Plenthy.

"You brought a wipper?" Plenthy said. "How unconventional!"

Jaq turned around and saw that the snake's head had reached the other end of his shelf. Its cold eyes locked on him. He quickly tied the rope around his waist and got ready to jump.

"Hand it to me, wipper," Plenthy said.

Bonip edged through the bars of the cage, and Plenthy grabbed the rope from the wipper's mouth and tied it to one of the bars of his cage.

"Young man!" cried Plenthy. "Swing off the shelf. I'll pull you up."

The snake was moving faster now, crossing the shelf and heading right for Jaq.

Jaq jumped just as the snake's tongue flicked out to taste him. He swung down and under the desk before swinging back up toward the bookshelf.

The snake had reached his jumping-off spot and was stretching his head out for Jaq.

Jaq tucked his legs into his body, ready to kick the snake's head if he swung too close, but his swing didn't make it back up to the shelf. He felt the rope yank.

There were *umph*s and *ugh*s coming from above, but Jaq didn't feel himself pulled toward the cage. He wrapped his foot around the rope and started climbing. He kept using his foot on the rope as a brake as he pulled himself higher and higher. At last, he reached the edge of the desk.

"Well done!" Plenthy cried as Jaq pulled himself over the edge. "I don't know what I was thinking. My muscles have completely atrophied in this cage."

Jaq rolled onto his back and took a few deep breaths. Then he got up and looked over the side of the desk. The snake had coiled itself back onto the shelf. "What do we do now?" he asked.

"The key to my cage is in that little cubby in the desk hutch," Plenthy said, pointing to the wooden storage unit that sat at the back side of the desk, nestled against the wall.

Jaq nodded. He ran around the cage and searched the square compartments until he found the key; then he ran back and opened the cage.

Plenthy stepped free.

"Bonip?" Jaq looked around. "Where are you?"

"Over here." Bonip was still in the cage, clinging to a brownish cube. It looked like he'd eaten half of it. "It's so gooooooooood."

"Freeze-dried worms," Plenthy said with a shudder. "They're disgusting. But if you eat them while reciting a poem by Florinxa Clow, they're passable."

Jaq saw more cubes by a round canister that had toppled over. He stuffed as many as he could into his backpack. "Let's get out of here," he said to Plenthy. "Maybe the two of us can move that door."

They lowered themselves to the floor, keeping an eye on the snake, who had twisted behind some boxes and was trying to turn itself around to get down.

Jaq looked at Plenthy. He had to be as old as Grandpa. Jaq remembered how heavy the door was and had a terrifying feeling that they wouldn't be able to escape.

When they got to the door, they both put their hands on it. "Ready?" Jaq said. "Push!"

The door barely moved . . . but it did move a little. Jaq kept looking back at the snake.

"Bonip, call the other wippers here," he said. "They can help from the other side."

"A hundred wippers couldn't budge this door," Plenthy said. "But you and I can do it. We just need to get into a rhythm."

Jaq pushed with all the panic and strength he had. He pushed and rested, pushed and rested, pushed and rested. Each time, the door opened a bit more. Even Bonip got off Jaq's shoulder to push.

"Next time, we run through."

They pushed, the door edged open, and they ran through, leaving the fearsome giant fang-toothed worm behind. Jaq's body flooded with relief.

But the moment was brief, because there in front of them were Morgo the (not so) Magnificent and Uncle Gunther, the extremely itchy and angry.

29

A PRISON OF HEARTBREAK

"HEY! WHY IS THAT DOOR SWINGING?" Gunther said.

The two giants hadn't seen the diminutive Yipsmixers on the floor yet.

"Someone's stealing my little man!" Morgo said. "There were three rival magicians at my last act. I knew they wanted to know how I did it!"

"No, you idiot," Gunther said. "It's Fiona—and that other little guy. He's come to rescue your prisoner. I knew Fiona was up to something. She never skateboards down this hall at night. She's lurking around here to help him! C'mon—let's look."

Plenthy pushed Jaq forward toward a stand-alone shelf of collars and clothes for pets. They jumped up onto the bottom shelf and wedged themselves behind a hanger of dog hats.

"He's gone!" they heard Morgo say from inside the office.

Jaq pressed himself back as far as he could go. The giant voices returned to the front room. "They could be hiding somewhere," Gunther said. "I'll check out here, you check back in there. And put that damn snake away before he eats your moneymaker!"

Thank Smolders for that, Jaq thought.

"He'll find us," Plenthy whispered. "It'll be back to the cage for me."

Jaq's body felt electric with panic. The thought of being a prisoner here was terrifying. Bonip crawled up to his shoulder.

Gunther was making a horrible racket as he threw things off the shelves to look behind them. He was going to reach their shelf soon, and Jaq and Plenthy would be sitting there like prize eggs at the annual egg hunt.

"Young man . . . I have a plan," Plenthy whispered, grabbing Jaq's arm. "I will distract the giant. You run for the door."

"I can't leave you now," Jaq said.

"And I cannot be responsible for your capture," Plenthy replied. "Please, I would rather stay here than risk your life."

Jaq couldn't say anything. He couldn't leave Plenthy behind to be recaptured by those cruel giants. The music Plenthy had played told Jaq exactly what Plenthy had been experiencing, and it was something no Yipsmixer should have to endure. The idea that Plenthy would sacrifice himself surrounded Jaq with walls of heartbreak. It was too much to feel, and Jaq felt a slow fury rise inside him.

"Wait for my signal," Plenthy said. "I want to make sure he's not looking your way."

"No, Plenthy, don't—"

But Plenthy had already eased himself out of their hiding place and disappeared around the shelf.

Jaq could see the blasts of color rising from where Gunther was searching. "Something has gotten into your stuff out here," his voice boomed. "Everything looks chewed by tiny mouths. Do you see anything?"

"My office has been ransacked!" Morgo's voice answered. "They could be hiding anywhere. You?"

"Not yet, but they can't have gotten far," Uncle Gunther

said. "The door was still swinging. I know they're in here somewhere."

"You got that right, Stinky!" Plenthy called out.

Jaq heard a crash and a yell from Gunther.

He grabbed Bonip and tried to follow the bursts of sound. He sprinted down the aisle until he reached the checkout counter near the front door. From here, he could see Plenthy on the top of a shelf, running away from Gunther.

Jaq felt like all the fears inside him were fighting each other—the fear of the giants, of the snake, of being captured, of seeing Plenthy get captured. He pushed them all down as he watched Gunther charge toward Plenthy.

"You can't get away, little man!" Gunther shouted. "And I'll find your friend, too! And when I do, I'm going to make him pay for what he did to me. My back is covered with itchy boils because of him. I'll make you both pay!"

"Bonip," Jaq said. "The other wippers are over by that wall." The wippers were chewing through boxes, and the sound made little jagged swishes of orange appear in Jaq's sight. "I have a plan. Tell them I'll give them enough freeze-dried worms to burst their bellies if they get over here now."

Bonip bounded off, soaring through the air with those tremendous hops.

Plenthy was still edging away from Gunther's approach. Jaq's heart ached at the sight of so much courage and sacrifice. He couldn't let Plenthy be captured again.

Gunther lunged for Plenthy, but Plenthy jumped out of his reach and across the top of the shelf. Jaq watched as Plenthy ran out of shelf, and Gunther scooped him up.

"Got him!" he yelled.

The back door opened, and Morgo stepped out. He was wearing the giant fang-toothed worm around his neck like a scarf. Jaq had never seen anything more terrifying.

"Where's the other one?" Morgo said.

"I don't know, but I have an idea on how to get him," Gunther said. "Hey! Little guy! Your friend here is going to be fed to the snake if you don't come out!"

Morgo smiled and nodded. "I've wanted to do that for weeks." He walked over to Gunther, holding the snake's head in his hand. Gunther held Plenthy tightly. Plenthy struggled, his eyes wide in panic. The snake's head came closer and closer.

The wippers bounded back to Jaq. As he leaned down to tell Bonip his plan, he couldn't take his gaze away from that snake and Plenthy's struggling form. The snake's tongue zipped out of its mouth to taste Plenthy.

Jaq couldn't take it any longer. "Stop!" he shouted, stepping into the aisle where the giants stood. "Put him down."

"No, Jaq!" Plenthy said. "Run!"

"Grab him, Gunther," Morgo said. "And then we'll feed the old guy to the snake."

"Wait—you said you wouldn't if I came out," Jaq said.

"I never promised that," Morgo said. "Gunther did. And it isn't Gunther's call. This little guy is worse than my mother for how much he nags me. I don't have to take it anymore. Gunther, give me Plenthy. You go get that kid."

Jaq watched as the elderly Yipsmixer twisted and writhed in his desperation to get free from Gunther's grip.

"No!" Jaq shouted. "Bonip, wippers—ATTACK!"

The scream startled Gunther, and he froze for a second. He looked around and saw nothing heading his way, so he laughed. "Nice try, mini-boy."

"Those bites you got yesterday," Jaq said, "were caused by one wipper. They're highly poisonous to your kind, as I'm sure you know. All that itching, all that nausea—caused by one little wipper. And there are now twelve wippers climbing up your socks. If you don't put Plenthy down, they will start biting. They will bite until I tell them to stop, and then they'll bite your friend."

"Grab him!" Morgo shouted. "Nothing so small could hurt you."

"Shut up, Morgo," Gunther said. "You don't know!"

Gunther was feeling itchy now—Jaq could tell. Gunther scratched his back with his free hand. He looked at his legs, lifting his pants. "I see them!"

"Put Plenthy down. Now!" Jaq shouted. Gunther madly scratched his legs with one hand while holding Plenthy with the other. Morgo bent down to look.

"They're tiny," Morgo said. "I'll get them with flea spray. Hold on."

"BITE!" Jaq commanded.

Gunther's eyes went wide. He dropped Plenthy so he could use both hands to scratch, but the wippers were gone from the itchy spot before his hands got close. Jaq knew from experience how wickedly fast they were. He watched Gunther spin and scratch. The giant screamed with frustration and pain as the wippers tore into him.

"I dropped him!" Gunther screamed. "Now make them stop!"

Jaq ran over to help Plenthy up; they both hustled for the door just as Morgo came back with a spray can in his hand.

"Attack the other giant!" Jaq yelled.

Jaq pushed Plenthy through the slot in the door. Gunther was still scratching like crazy, unaware that the biting had stopped. Morgo tried to spray Gunther's legs, but it was difficult because Gunther was jumping around like a madman. His legs probably felt like they were on fire. And then Morgo turned the spray on himself as he felt the stinging attack of the wippers climbing up the inside of his pants.

"Bonip! Wippers! Now!" Jaq called. He watched the wippers crawl out the bottom of Morgo's pants and bound toward him. He caught the first one in the air and eased it through the slot.

"It's so nice to be caught," the next wipper said when he landed in Jaq's hands. "Thanks."

Quickly, his heart in a panic, Jaq caught and lifted the wippers through the slot, counting them as he did. He turned to look at the giants. Gunther had stripped off his shirt, and Jaq saw that he was covered with blistering red dots. Morgo took a break from spraying his ankle to spray Gunther's back.

"OUCH! That stings! Stop it!" Gunther swung his arms at Morgo, clocking him on the side of the head, which enraged Morgo, who swung at Gunther.

Jaq jumped through the slot.

"They're getting away!" Morgo yelled.

✳

In the hallway, Fiona scooped up Jaq in one hand. The other hand held Plenthy. The wippers clung to her pants, the way they had earlier. She pushed off on her skateboard just as the pet store door burst open.

"There they are!"

Jaq turned and saw Morgo dash out of the pet store. He was so close, but Fiona was faster on her skateboard, and they zoomed away.

"You'd better stop or else!" Morgo yelled after them.

Fiona reached the intersection and then turned the wrong way. Instead of going left—toward the moving staircase and safety—she went right.

"Where are you going?" Jaq yelled.

"I need to draw them away from the wormhole," she said. "You don't want them to find out where you guys came from. Hang on!"

They were moving so fast, but Fiona seemed sure-footed on her wheeled board. Jaq watched Morgo chasing after them, but he was falling farther behind. Gunther had probably been immobilized by itchiness and nausea back at the pet store.

Fiona stopped at the top of a staircase. She put Plenthy on

her shoulder, picked up the board, and raced down the stairs to the lower level. "Now we'll head to the wormhole. But first I'm going to open the back door. Maybe they'll think I left. Plus, it will set off the alarm, and the police will come."

At the lower level, Fiona opened the glass door. "He can't hurt me if the police are here. My mom will kill me for getting us kicked out of his place, though." She got back on her board and pushed off.

"Don't worry!" Jaq yelled as they zoomed toward the fountain. "I brought the diamonds. They're buried by the wormhole."

"Really?"

They reached the fountain. As soon as Fiona stopped, Jaq jumped off and ran for the bushes. He quickly dug up his bundle of diamonds and brought them out for Fiona.

"Ah! Well done, Jaq," Plenthy said.

"Wow. Wow, wow, wow!" Fiona said in awe. "There are so many! Thank you, Jaq." Fiona clutched the small bundle.

Jaq looked at the wormhole, ready to rush for it, but first he turned to Fiona. "Are you going to be okay?" he asked.

"My mom will be here soon, and the police, too. Gunther can't do anything to me."

"Guess again," a deep voice said. Gunther jumped out

SHEILA GRAU

of the bushes and grabbed Fiona. "I knew you'd head back here."

"Let her go!" Plenthy screamed.

"Not until I see what you little creeps gave her," Gunther replied, trying to pry Fiona's hand open with one hand while tightly holding her other arm so she couldn't get away. He became a spastic display of reaching for Fiona's hand, then releasing it to scratch, then grabbing her again, over and over.

Fiona looked terrified. Jaq froze, then looked at Plenthy for help. The elder Yipsmixer shook his head.

"Just what do you think you're doing, Gunther?"

Jaq looked behind him and saw another giant walking toward them.

"Mom!" Fiona yelled.

"Let her go," Fiona's mom said. "Or I'll have you arrested for assault."

Gunther's face twisted in anger, and for a moment it seemed like he wasn't going to let her go. But when Fiona's mom walked over to him and grabbed her daughter, he released her.

"What's going on?" Fiona's mom said.

Gunther pointed a finger at Fiona. "She's a complete

224

delinquent," he said. "She skateboards around like she owns the place, she set off the mall alarm, and she destroyed a pet store upstairs. You are going to have to pay, and pay big."

They argued, with Fiona trying to explain and Gunther interrupting. More commotion followed as the police arrived to see why the mall's alarm had sounded, and Gunther had to rush over to them to explain that everything was fine.

Fiona's mom looked at her daughter. "Fiona? Tell the truth, did you destroy that pet store?"

"No, Mom," she said. "I didn't destroy the pet store. They did." She pointed to Jaq and the wippers.

Jaq waved at Fiona's mom, whose jaw dropped open at the sight of the small Yipsmixers.

Plenthy stepped forward. "Madam, it is thanks to your daughter's heroic efforts that we were able to escape from the pet store manager, Mortimer, who is not only a sadistic maniac but also a terrible magician. We have rewarded her with a collection of diamonds from our planet. But we really must get back. I just checked the wormhole, and it's nearly vanished."

"Yes, we have to go now," Jaq said. "Good–bye, Fiona. I'll never forget you."

"And I'll never forget you two, too." She smiled and crouched down, putting a hand around each Yipsmixer.

Jaq hugged her hand and then turned to Plenthy. "Let's go."

The wippers led the way into the bushes, and together they all approached the wormhole.

"Oh, Smolders, I hope this thing still works," Jaq said.

They dove in.

30

WHEN THE GREAT SMOLDERS CLOSES A DOOR, SOMETIMES HE OPENS A WORMHOLE

T HEY ALL FAINTED UPON COMING OUT of the wormhole and didn't wake up until much later, when Jaq's sense of time told him that it was morning.

Jaq woke first, in the dark. He flicked on his flashlight and saw the bodies of Plenthy and the wippers next to him. The shimmering oval was gone.

Jaq shook Plenthy, and the older man woke with a start. "Great Smolders, that was a terrible transfer." He sat up and looked around. "It's gone, isn't it?"

"Yes," Jaq said. "It used to be right there. Bonip, are you okay?"

Bonip lay facedown in the dirt. "Ouch," he said. "Can't move."

The rest of the wippers woke up with grumbles and shoves. Wippers are very cranky in the morning.

"Guys?" Jaq said. "I have something for you." He pulled two brownish cubes out of his backpack. "Morgo called these freeze-dried worms—" he began to explain, but he didn't get the chance to finish because the wippers had charged him to get at the cubes.

"Wippers," Plenthy said, shaking his head. "Little gluttons."

"You guys were amazing," Jaq told the wippers, who were now bouncing up and down with pleasure, stuffing their faces and laughing.

"Ugh, those giants tasted terrible," one said. "But what fun!"

"Did you hear him scream? That was my bite, I'm sure of it."

"I bite deeper," another said. "And my poison's been known to bring down a full-grown gow."

Plenthy stood up, stretching his arms. "Ah! Freedom!

Fantastic freedom. You have no idea of the tortures that man put me through. The racket in that pet shop was unbearable. I told him I needed to compose music to keep my sanity. I didn't think my message would work, though."

"It took me a while to figure it out."

"I have to tell you, young man, I wasn't optimistic when I saw you in the bushes. *Greggin sent a kid?* I thought. But you are a very brave kid." He patted Jaq on the shoulder.

"Thanks," Jaq said.

"How is my old friend?" Plenthy asked. "Why wasn't he able to come himself?"

"He hasn't been the same since you left with all his money," Jaq said. "You . . . you ruined him. You took his money, and his friend's money, and disappeared. Vilcot thought the two of you had swindled him, and he made my grandpa sell his farm to pay him back. Vilcot has been making our lives miserable ever since."

"Oh no," Plenthy said.

"And now Grandpa is in jail, and we have no money," Jaq went on. "But I got a key from someone named Dharvil Meyr." He fished it out of his backpack and showed the note to Plenthy. "Does this mean you're rich? Does it mean you can you save our farm?"

Plenthy didn't seem to be listening. He was reading the note. "My dream is so close . . . ," he said.

"What dream?" Jaq asked.

"My dream of everyone being able to afford a glug room. Every house should have one. Why should only rich people enjoy that luxury, hmm? It's a necessity, if you ask me. Everyone needs a place to escape the noise of life. I've spent decades trying to figure out how to make this dream a reality."

The wippers had finished off the worm cubes and were climbing over Jaq to get at his backpack. He opened it up and put the last cube on the ground.

"After I found the wormhole," Plenthy went on, "I asked myself—why is glug so cheap on Earth? The answer—because it grows on trees! Money literally grows on trees there. Well, not *on* trees, but *in* them.

"I took your grandfather's money and his friend's money, and I bought a ranch in Coocoovox. I cleared the fields and began the process of trying to grow sapodilla trees on Yipsmix. It was very difficult work, because trees are so much larger on Earth. Oh, it's a long story, and I ache all over."

"Are you saying that my grandfather can get his money back?" Jaq asked.

"He could, but why would he want to?" Plenthy said. "Your grandfather is now the one-third owner of a glug farm. A very successful glug farm. Your grandfather, that Vilcot fellow, and I were equal owners, but if your grandfather bought out Vilcot, well, then, he's actually twice as rich as me!" Plenthy smiled. "And I am quite rich, my boy. And now I'm free! Oh, glorious day!"

Rich? Grandpa was rich? Jaq fell backward and let the words cover him like a blanket of happiness. They wouldn't have to move. They could save their farm. They could buy food.

But Jaq had been happy before, and he didn't quite trust this happy feeling. He knew from experience that the Vilcots would find a way of snatching that blanket off him and leaving him cold once again.

The exhausted space travelers trudged down the hill and headed for the marketplace. Jaq could barely move his limbs, mostly because they were covered with wippers who preferred clinging to him to walking on their own. He didn't care. He was dirty and dusty, his clothing more torn than usual, but a spark of excitement kept him moving. He'd saved Plenthy . . . Plenthy was rich . . . And now Grandpa was, too.

"I don't get it. How did you do it?" Jaq asked. "How do you grow glug in trees?"

"It's in the sap, my boy. And it wasn't easy, let me tell you. Earthers no longer get their glug from trees; they make it in factories, like us. I couldn't replicate their factories; we don't have the raw materials for that. But I thought I might be able to replicate their tree-sap gum on Yipsmix.

"I had a great number of failures," Plenthy said. "I had to figure out which type of tree produces gum and then track it down. I can't believe Greggin knew nothing of this. I sent reports to his farm."

"I told you, he sold his farm, and then Vilcot bought it. Vilcot probably threw out anything from you."

"Ah, well, after I learned the techniques of bonsai, which is a way to make trees grow smaller through careful pruning of the plant and its roots, I was able to grow a whole orchard of Earth trees on Yipsmix. I've had to reinvest most of the proceeds—hiring people to tend the trees while I was away, that sort of thing. I was about to pay out our company's first dividend to your grandfather and his friend when I was captured by Morgo."

"Fiona told me that glug that goes through the wormhole turns to dust," Jaq said.

"That's true."

"What about the diamonds I gave Fiona? Will they turn to dust?"

"Diamonds are the fifth-strongest mineral in the universe—that we know of," Plenthy said. "They'll be fine."

✳

Gift-giving is common throughout worlds, although each world has its own rules of etiquette. There are many occasions when one might want to give a gift: to show that you care about someone, to celebrate a milestone in someone's life, or to thank someone for rescuing you from a life of performing in cheesy magic acts.

On Epsidor Erandi, gift-giving has evolved into a very straightforward activity. Everyone on that planet has collected a large stack of gift cards, and now people just pass them around as occasions arise. There have been no documented cases of a gift card actually being redeemed on Epsidor Erandi.

On Zanflid, there are only three ways to communicate your thanks to another person. The first method is to say the words *Thank you*. If that seems inadequate, the grateful person might choose to elevate his thanks to the second level—he or she will grab the shoulders of the thankee, look that person straight in the eye, and say, with extra emphasis and sincerity, "Thank you."

The third level of thanks occurs when a person is completely overcome with gratitude at another person's generosity or thoughtfulness. In this case, a hug is given. But, honestly, this just embarrasses everyone and is often fodder for humiliating stories at family dinners.

On Earth, gift-giving traditions are as varied as they are confusing. And on Yipsmix, there are rules about inappropriate gifts. You would never give someone tap-dancing shoes, for instance, because the sound of metallic clacking tastes like rotten eggs.

Yorlim Plenthy wanted to thank Jaq for rescuing him and saving his life. As soon as they reached the marketplace, Plenthy turned to Jaq. "Let me pop in here," he said, pointing to the bank. "I'll be right out."

Jaq nodded. He looked down at his gang of happy wippers. "Guys, if you want to head home, I'll meet you there."

Hedgemud nodded. "That's a good idea. Wippers aren't real welcome at the marketplace, I've found. We'll head back to your farm, Jaq. And we'll be waiting to hear what happens with your family. We're pulling for you, kid."

"Thanks."

"You guys go ahead," Bonip said. "I'll stay with Jaq."

The wippers left, bouncing with happy springs down the road. Jaq sat down on a bench. It was a quiet time in the marketplace, too early for most shoppers. A few people sat at outdoor tables, eating breakfast. Others strolled by on soft shoes that didn't clatter in explosions of color. Jaq felt so comfortable in the soft sepia tones of his planet.

"You did good back there," Bonip said. "It was real brave of you to face those giants like that."

"Me? You guys did all the work," Jaq said, and Bonip smiled.

Jaq was just starting to feel a little hungry when Plenthy came out waving a piece of paper. "Your grandfather's first dividend check," he said. "And it's a doozy! He's going to be so surprised."

Jaq stood up, smiling. He thought about asking Plenthy if he could spare a few damars for a saltmint drink and a cakie. Cakies are like cookies, only gooier. Rich kids bring them to school on their birthdays, and Jaq loved them.

"What do you say you ride home in style?" Plenthy asked. He nodded toward the hoverbike showroom.

Jaq's eyes went wide. "Really?"

Plenthy put an arm around him. "Pick out any bike you want. It'll be my gift to you, for rescuing me."

Jaq knew *exactly* which one he wanted. The Zipley Roadster with Hushed Drive and Turbo Boosters.

"What about me?" Bonip asked. "I'm hungry."

"How can you be hungry?" Jaq said. "You just ate."

Plenthy laughed. "Wippers, ha! Listen, while I pay for the bike, why don't you two run out and get yourselves some breakfast?" He handed Jaq a huge wad of damars and nodded toward the door.

Jaq bought his favorite drink and a cakie, and one for Bonip, and two more for his mom and grandpa. They sat down on a bench to wait for Plenthy. Jaq sipped his drink, letting Bonip take licks of the whipped cream on top.

"Yum," Bonip said.

Jaq was so happy. But as soon as he realized that, he knew it was only a matter of time before a Vilcot showed up. It was like they were equipped with happiness detectors: Whenever they sensed a happy Rollop, they'd swoop in to squash him.

Right on schedule, Jaq looked up to see Tormy Vilcot coming right for him.

Bonip ducked behind Jaq's collar.

"Hey, loser," Tormy said. He held a bag from the candy store and took out a giant piece of string candy, slurping it with a loud smacking noise.

"Tormy, if you ever stop being such a jerk, you might actually like yourself a little bit," Jaq said.

"Good one," Bonip whispered in his ear.

"Shut up," Tormy said. "At least I'm not poor."

"You're right, I am poor," Jaq said. "But I wouldn't take a million damars if it meant I had to be you."

"Yeah? Well, who would give you a million damars anyway? You Rollops can't do anything."

"Like your homework?" Jaq said. "That was your first one hundred percent, wasn't it? The homework that I did for you."

"Shut up. I don't need to do good in school. My dad's rich."

"Right. Well, I'm not doing your homework for you anymore." It felt so good to say that, to finally stand up to Tormy and watch that arrogant smirk melt off his face. Jaq stood up, smiling. "See you."

"Not for much longer!" Tormy yelled after him. "Don't forget—you have to move out by nightfall tonight. We're going to own it all now. Everything! And then you'll be left with nothing, which is more than you deserve."

Jaq ignored him. He couldn't wait to tell his mother and grandfather the good news.

He hadn't taken two steps away from Tormy when a man

came up to him, dragging a floating hoverbike behind him. "Jaq Rollop? Here's your new bike. Your friend told me he would meet you later at the farm. He has other business to attend to."

"Thanks!" Jaq hopped onto the hoverbike and took a brief moment to savor the look of utter shock on Tormy's face as he whispered, "That's a Zipley Roadster." Then Jaq was off. He rode past the fountain and saw the same look of shock on Davardi's face. It was fantastic.

"Thanks for the key!" Jaq yelled at Davardi as he passed him.

31

ENDINGS ARE LIKE CAKIES—SWEET AND OVER TOO SOON

JAQ AND BONIP FLEW HOME. JAQ RODE HIS hoverbike right over the fence and up to his front door. He ran inside to find the room empty.

There was a note on the table.

Jaq—You're going to have to spend the night alone, I'm afraid. I've got a lead on someone in Shimporti City who might lend us the money we need to pay off Vilcot. I'll be back in the morning.

Love, Mom

Jaq put the note down and sat in the chair, relieved that his mother hadn't spent the night worrying about where he was. Bonip was already fast asleep on the floor. Jaq closed his eyes and felt the exhaustion of the past few days overtake him.

He wasn't sure how long he'd been asleep when the angry voice of his grandfather woke him up.

"We've got until sundown, you no-good, greedy, arrogant fool— Oh, it's you, Jaq. There's a fancy hoverbike outside. I thought it belonged to Vilcot."

"Grandpa, you're out of jail!"

"They kicked me out," Grandpa said. "Can you believe that? I wanted to stay, but they made me leave."

"Jaq," his mother said, coming in behind Grandpa. "I'm so sorry I had to leave you alone. Have you had breakfast? Why don't you grab a plate and see what you can scrape off it."

"You're a mess," Grandpa said. "Go find your spare shirt."

"It doesn't matter," Jaq said, jumping up and smiling so wide, he thought his face was going to split. "We're rich! I found Plenthy. Grandpa, he didn't swindle you. He's been building a glug farm with your investment. It's a huge success!"

Grandpa couldn't speak. Jaq's mom couldn't speak. They looked at him as if he were talking in a different language. Jaq handed them each a cakie while he explained, telling them everything that had happened. His mom kept saying, "It can't be true," like she was scared to be hopeful, because their hopes were always crushed.

Jaq gave his grandfather the key that had saved them. Grandpa still had the first key, and he kissed them both.

"I knew I could trust that Plenthy," Grandpa said. "Good man, good man."

The door burst open again, and this time Tormy Vilcot and his grandfather barged in, followed by Davardi.

"You stole my key!" the elder Vilcot bellowed. He walked right up to Jaq and yelled in his face. "You have my key and I want it back."

"That's funny," Jaq said to Davardi, who was standing behind Vilcot. "When I wanted my wipper-slinger back, you said, 'A deal is a deal.'"

"That's right," Grandpa said. He stood up slowly and walked over to the elder Vilcot, poking him in the chest. "You've already taken everything you're entitled to and then some. How can you possibly think we owe you anything more?"

"Because you robbed me!" Vilcot swatted the finger away from his chest. "You tricked me. You have to be punished."

"I did not trick you. And I paid my debt in full. With my farm. You lost nothing, and yet you still act like you're the victim."

"You should be in jail."

"What more do you want from me?" Grandpa asked.

"I want those keys!" Vilcot screamed.

"Well, I want my farm!" Grandpa screamed back.

The two men stared at each other. Jaq could feel the invisible current of hatred that seemed to flow between them. He felt it charge and grow, the air pulsing. It frightened him.

"Why don't you trade?" he said.

The current disappeared as they both looked at him.

"Grandpa, you can give him the keys . . . and Vilcot can sell us our farm back. We can pay him whatever he paid for it. Then everyone's got what they started with. That's a fair deal."

Grandpa clutched the keys a little tighter. Vilcot looked suspicious.

Jaq shrugged. "Fine, you two can keep wanting what the other has."

"I don't know if I want my farm back. He's ruined it," Grandpa said. "Have you seen the dying vines? And he sold off all my animals." He held up the key. "With this, I can probably buy that huge spread over in Upper Chumplex."

"No," said Vilcot. "The only way to make things right is to go back to how we were. I'll give you your farm back if you pay me what I paid for it, plus interest, and the keys. Everything should be back with its original owner."

"Then I get Klingdux back," Jaq said. "And my plastic bird with the glugballs."

"No way," Tormy sneered.

"Tormy!" Vilcot hushed his grandson. Then he whispered in his ear: "They've had those keys for two days and have come back with more glug than I've seen in my life. They've bought themselves a Zipley Roadster, and they've offered to pay me more than the farm is now worth."

Tormy glanced outside at the Roadster. He sneered and said to Jaq, "Fine. You can take the stupid critter, for all I care."

"But we will not return the chicken," Vilcot said. "That's not part of the agreement. You can forget this deal if you demand the plastic bird. And the glug display I've set up in our trophy room stays with us, too."

Grandpa squinted at Vilcot as if he were unable to make a deal with the man he hated. But at last he said, "All right."

"Not so fast. First tell me how the key works," Vilcot said.

"The key splits apart," Jaq said. "There was a map inside. It led to a wormhole, which is like a tunnel through space. On Earth, glug is everywhere."

"Everywhere?"

"That glug-filled chicken cost less on Earth than a drink at Cinaco's Refreshments," Jaq said. "People spit glug out onto sidewalks, stick it under tables, and treat it like garbage. It grows in trees there."

Vilcot rubbed his fingers together; they were itching to grab the keys.

"Show me the map," Vilcot demanded.

Jaq took the key from Grandpa and opened it. Jaq had put the now-worthless map back inside. He didn't tell Vilcot that the map was worthless, that the wormhole was gone. He felt a little guilty about holding on to that information, because he knew he was tricking Vilcot the same way he'd been tricked.

"On the other side is a letter to Grandpa from Plenthy,

asking for help," Jaq said. "He'd been sending updates to Grandpa at the farm. Why didn't you forward the mail to Grandpa?"

"Help you miscreants? Ha! Never. The day I help a Rollop is a day the moons collide. I threw all those letters out."

Vilcot really wasn't making it easy to do the right thing.

"Nobody swindled you," Jaq said. "If you'd have just been patient, you'd be part owner of a glug farm."

"Stop talking. You're just a kid and you don't know anything," Vilcot said. "Glug farm . . . Do you think I was born yesterday?"

"The glug farm is real," a voice said. Jaq looked over and saw Plenthy coming through the front door. He was wearing new clothes, and Jaq could see that Davardi wanted to reach out to feel how soft they were. "You would be a part owner if you hadn't gotten nervous and demanded your money back."

"You!" Vilcot said.

"Yes, me. And yes, I've been away too long. But I've been working very hard to make this investment pay off. And it has. Our glug farm has produced enough glug to pave the streets from here to the marketplace."

"Hmm . . . I think I'll put a swimming pool in over there,"

Grandpa said, pointing to the dead ripweed field. "And turn this shack into a gazebo. Then I'll get my animals back—the robuses, the caponutters, and, of course, the gows."

"Do what you want, you old fool," Vilcot said. "This smelly pit hole of a town was never good enough for a Vilcot. With what you're paying for the farm, plus all our new glug, we'll be able to move out of here for good."

The Vilcots left to get the farm deed so the deal could be finalized. Grandpa couldn't stop smiling after they were gone, and he and Plenthy talked and talked like the old friends they were. Grandpa's whole demeanor had changed dramatically with the return of his friend. His slothful disposition had disappeared, replaced by an almost childlike excitement, an excitement that was bolstered considerably when Plenthy showed him the dividend check. Plenthy also agreed to lend the Rollops whatever they'd need to buy the farm back.

When Vilcot returned, he signed over the deed in exchange for the checks. Then he looked at Jaq, who held the keys.

Jaq looked at his grandfather. His grandfather seemed to know what Jaq was thinking, because he just nodded.

"Wait," Jaq said. "I have to tell you something. These keys are worthless. The wormhole is gone. You can't go back to

Earth. But you're still getting a fair price for the farm, even without the keys."

The elder Vilcot frowned at Jaq. "You trying to get out of our deal? We had an agreement. If you don't hand over those keys, I'll take you to court."

"Okay, fine," Jaq said. "But I still want Klingdux."

"Tormy!" Vilcot yelled.

Tormy came in holding Jaq's pet, who was twisting and turning to get out of his grip.

"Take the stupid creature!" he yelled, tossing Klingdux to the ground.

Jaq scooped him up, laughing as Klingdux licked his cheeks. He held out the keys to Vilcot, who snatched them out of his hand and left.

It was over. Jaq had Klingdux back, and his grandfather had his farm back.

✳

The Rollops knew that Vilcot wouldn't take the disappearance of the wormhole well, and, sure enough, the very next day they saw an angry Vilcot storm into the marketplace, his eyes blazing with fury.

He spotted the Rollops at the outdoor café and charged up to them, throwing the worthless keys on the table.

"You swindled me."

"You swindled yourself," Grandpa said very calmly. "Vilcot, if you'd just believed me from the beginning, if you'd just trusted our friendship, we'd all be rich and happy right now. But no, your pride and greed got the better of you."

"This isn't over," Vilcot said, pointing a finger at each Rollop in turn. "Nobody makes a fool of me."

"Nobody was trying to," Grandpa said. "You do a fine job of it on your own."

EPILOGUE

I was a nice gazebo. Winnowberry vines crawled up the frame and draped the top with pretty pale yellow flowers. Sitting in the shade underneath, Jaq watched the streaks of red and blue that flew and swished through the sky with each yell of a flying wipper. Bonip, sitting in his own mini-chair, slurped up worms from a bucket next to him.

"Ahhhhh!" a flying wipper screamed.

Jaq smiled as the wipper landed in the middle of the swimming pool with a tiny splash.

"Eight point five!" Bonip shouted.

"Nine! That was a nine!" another said. The other wippers all called out their scores.

Grandpa and Plenthy sat next to Jaq, sipping tendamelon tea. "Look at that," Grandpa said, pointing to Klingdux. The fence was gone, and they could see right into an orchard of fruit trees, where Klingdux picked up the next wipper, spun in a whirl, and let him fly. "Wippers playing with a wipper-slinger. Who'd have thought?"

"Bonip did," Jaq said, smiling down at his friend. "After

Klingdux flung him over here before I left that last time. He said that Klingdux wasn't such a bad guy after all. He was just doing what came naturally."

"Smart wipper, that Bonip," said Plenthy.

"Hold on," Jaq said, pointing at the sky. A small body flew through the air. It looked like a kid, only wipper-sized. "That's not a wipper."

The miniature girl caught sight of Jaq and yelled *"Erip nu!"* right before she splashed into the water.

"Erip nu?" Grandpa repeated. "She's not from around here, is she?"

"Grandpa, she's as small as a wipper. Of course she's not from around here."

"Hot tamales!" Plenthy said, jumping up. "Looks like someone found another wormhole."